Secret Places
of the Stairs

Secret Places of the Stairs

by Susan Sallis

1 8 17

HARPER & ROW, PUBLISHERS

Cambridge, Philadelphia, San Francisco, London, Mexico City, São Paulo, Sydney

NEW YORK

Designed by Joyce Hopkins
1 2 3 4 5 6 7 8 9 10
FIRST EDITION

Library of Congress Cataloging in Publication Data
Sallis, Susan.
    Secret places of the stairs.

    "A Charlotte Zolotow book."
    Summary: Seventeen-year-old Cass misunderstands her
divorced parents until she discovers the secret they've
been keeping from her: she has a severely handicapped,
terminally ill younger sister.
    [1. Sisters—Fiction.   2. Divorce—Fiction.
3. Down's syndrome—Fiction.   4. Physically handicapped—
Fiction.   5. Handicapped—Fiction]   I. Title.
PZ7.S1533Se 1984   [Fic]   83-48442
ISBN 0-06-025142-5
ISBN 0-06-025147-6 (lib. bdg.)

Secret Places
of the Stairs

Is a detective story about discovering secrets? Stripping off layer upon layer of them until you come to what you think is the truth?

If it is, then this is a detective story and I must be careful to take off one layer at a time. That's tricky, because I'm at the end of the story right now, and it's a temptation to write that first and fill in the middle afterward. But if I do that, Nadine and Gideon and the Lavender Lady might seem irrelevant. And they weren't irrelevant. Without them I might not even have known that the secret places of the stairs existed. Without them I could never have peeled off the layers.

Without them . . . well, I can't imagine much without them.

Nadine was always there. At least she was there when I left my primary school in the Mendip Hills and went to the big comprehensive down near Dundry. She was still there when I went to the College of Further Education to learn how to be a super secretary. When things got a bit hairy at home, I went to stay with her. And when she'd had her mum and dad and their pub at Westbury right up to her eyebrows, she came out to the farm and stayed with us. Dad thought she was mad, but he got on well with her; Dad's wife, Betty, didn't know what to think of her. Dad and Betty's kids, the terrible twins, Jack and Jenny, went mad with delight when she entered the door. She livened the place up.

A couple of times I took her to Weston for a weekend to stay with my mum and her husband and their son. That wasn't so good. We tended to eat breakfast and supper at the big house along the front, then skive off into Weston to see what life had to offer.

Anyway, I was staying with Nadine at the Dying Duck the first time we saw the Lavender Lady, so I'll start there. It was spring vacation. Nadine's mum had asked us to get a loaf of bread—cheap offer— from the hypermarket. It was raining. It was midday.

Nadine said, "Christ. If she didn't want a penny off every blasted thing, we could have got it in the village."

I pulled the hood of my duffel up and spoke in a dramatic monotone. "The girls hurried toward the fallout shelter. Wind whipped radioactive cigarette packs against their microaluminum-covered legs. People stared admiringly at them as they adjusted their helmets, and the word went around that they were on a rescue mission. Mission fairies."

Nadine said gloomily, "Yeah. It looks like a blasted fallout shelter stuck in the middle of a bomb site. And what's microaluminum?"

"The stuff our radioactive suits are made of. All shiny and sexy."

"Very funny. Mission fairies. Most amusing." Nadine did not laugh and I dried up.

Two women passed us shoving a cart with a kid inside it. The kid was bound up like in those pictures of Chinese refugees. Its small exposed face was covered in snot. The one woman was adjusting and re-adjusting her head scarf, and as they passed us, we could see that her upraised arms had lifted her plastic jacket away from the top of her jeans. The revealed slice of spine was covered with hair.

Nadine said, "*Planet of the Apes?*"

At last we giggled. We couldn't stop. In the green-house heat of the market some maverick carts waltzed slowly by themselves. I got one, shoved the handle at Nadine, climbed in and folded myself up. I pushed back my hood, finger combed my hair till it stood on end, spat on my hands and scrubbed my face, stuck a thumb in my mouth and cried.

Nadine picked up her cue instantly. She straightened her face and pushed the cart briskly through the automatic doors. Two men in smart blazers with names in their lapels lounged by Lloyd's Cashpoint. "Stop crying, baby-darling-Mummy's-precious," cooed Nadine. "We're just coming to the sweeties." The men looked sharply at me and moved unobtrusively in our wake. I let out a howl like a werewolf at full moon and Nadine went on glutinously, "No more nice drinkies of blood today, darling." The men exchanged glances and one fell back. The other leaned against a vacant checkout and watched us head for the bakery.

The female apes were there cogitating the advantages of a large cake at thirty-nine pence as against a frozen medium-sliced at thirty and a half. Nadine edged me close to their sticky kid, who stared at me with a lack of expression that was chilling.

"Now, now, darling, don't touch the nice cakies," Nadine cooed, slapping at my hand quite hard. She smiled at the woman with the hairy spine. "I never know where her fingers have been."

The two women turned and surveyed me with the same lack of expression as the kid. I replaced my thumb and dribbled around it and made mewling noises. One of the women said, "I 'ad a cousin like that. Used to wet 'isself all the time. Got 'im in a 'ome in the finish." She fished in her pocket and produced a furry jelly baby. " 'Ave this, dearie. Nicer than that dirty ole thumb, eh?" She forcibly lowered my hand and shoved the sticky sweet into my astonished mouth. I spat vigorously into my hanky.

The women were furious.

"Some sort of joke is it? You should be bloody thankful you've got all your marbles instead of messin' about pretendin' otherwise! Great girls like you too. Should know better."

Nadine appeared to be having a convulsion but she managed to remove me to the privacy of the dress racks.

"They thought you were a nutter!" she spluttered. "*Them!* They thought you were mental! They—"

"Never mind that." The joke had gone stale for me and my feet were hurting. "Help me out, you moron—and do something with this rotten sweet! And stop that silly *tittering*!"

She couldn't. She fell over the handle of the cart and I went down again and that made her worse. Spluttering helplessly, she parked me by a freezer full of cheeses.

"Hang on. I'll get the bread. . . . Oh, my God, if you could see your face . . . oh, my God . . ." She staggered away. I crouched again and ground my teeth. The freezer was surrounded by a dozen or so people. They glanced at me, then quickly away. I could have murdered Nadine.

There was one way to get my own back. I looked furtively to left and right with very obvious cunning. Then I reached out and picked up a cheese and began to gnaw at the clear plastic covering. It would serve

Nadine right. She'd have to pay for the cheese, and if she tried to expose me, I'd bawl so loud no one would hear her puny excuses.

Incredibly, nobody seemed to notice my chewing. I made a growling sound in my throat and gnashed at the impregnable plastic. There were antitheft mirrors everywhere, yet no one came for me. Nadine hove into sight clutching a loaf. She saw me and quickened her step, but she was still giggling and didn't negotiate the intervening carts too well. I hung my head over the cheese to hide my own grin, and a voice said above me with enormous and kindly surprise, "My dear! Whatever are you doing here?"

A gloved hand smelling of lavender appeared in front of my down-bent face, and suddenly the voice became artificial. "Dearie! How did you know I needed cheese?" The hand took the cheese from me and I looked up with it to see a powdered lady in a fur hat smiling ever-so-brightly at the man with the name in his lapel. "Isn't she a clever girl? Double Gloucester too—my favorite!" The man eyed the fur hat, the matching fur coat, got the redolence of lavender and pound notes and moved off. The woman said quietly, "Dearie, you really shouldn't—" Then she got a good look at my face and blanched. "Oh, it's not . . . oh, I am *so* sorry! I thought you were someone else! How silly of me—I do apologize!"

Nadine arrived hotfoot and snatched at the cart. There were some breathless words, the loaf was shown. We left the Lavender Lady clutching the mangled Double Gloucester and made for the checkout.

That was the first time I saw the Lavender Lady.

I went home the next day. I let myself in and Betty heard me and came dashing out of the kitchen to give me a welcome. It's the sort of thing that makes me feel like a visitor.

"Hello, Cass." She took my duffel and hung it on a hanger. "Had a good time? Were you warm enough? Where are your gloves?"

"Pocket."

She felt in my pocket, removed the damp gloves and put them on the radiator.

"How was Nadine? And Mrs. Miller?"

"Okay. Fine. Where's Dad?"

"Sheep pens. More lambs already." She laughed and moved her head on her rigid neck in a way she had. It made her small chin disappear into her throat. "I'm just making tea. Will you have some?"

"Thanks. Lovely. Jenny and Jack all right?"

"Oh, yes. They've been in all day with this rain, and there's a bit of a mess. . . . Won't you go into the living room, dear?"

I didn't bother to reply. If she thought I was going to sit in the living room with a cup of tea while she and Dad and the twins had theirs in the kitchen . . .

It was gloriously chaotic. Saucepan lids all over the floor. Jennifer advancing toward me with upraised rolling pin, Jacqueline bare from the waist down, squatting on her pot. Betty was flustered right up to her stiff neck and started to tidy up. I took the rolling pin away from Jen and swung her into the air. She yelled and Betty removed her. The kettle started to whistle on the stove.

I sat down on a stool and let it all happen. It was the way she wanted it, after all. Jenny went on yelling, and Betty tried to make the tea with her under one arm, and Jack bounced up and down and informed us that her job had been done. An atrocious smell bore this out.

The cacophony had reached a climax when the door to the yard opened and Dad came in. Jacqueline stood up. "Dada!" she announced and kicked the potty and its contents into a saucepan lid. Betty let out a scream that drowned Jennifer's. Dad scooped Jacqueline under one arm, picked up the fouled saucepan lid and threw it into the sink, took Jennifer from Betty with his free hand and sank onto the stool opposite mine.

Everything was suddenly quiet.

He said, "So . . . you're home, are you?"

It was the way he said it. What he meant was "immediately you walk through the door, everything happens and you don't do anything about it."

I smiled widely at him. "Yes." The single word dropped into the silence like a knell. I stood up and made for the hall door. "Thanks for the welcome," I said lightly. "It's marvelous to be back."

I went upstairs to my room.

Betty had picked three enormous bunches of forsythia and arranged them in her inimitable style in jam jars around my room. As if we didn't have any vases. I opened the window onto the icy wind funneling down through the Cheddar Gorge and dropped them delicately onto the neatly truncated stalks of last year's chrysanths. Betty would see them there quite soon, because she was always working in the garden. She was in her element there. That's why she'd come originally, to help Dad with the outside work. I managed indoors okay with help from Mrs. Tossell, but I'd never liked the real rough stuff on the farm. Betty did. She'd be out soon looking for snowdrops and primroses.

I put my stuff away, turned the radiator up full and sat down in front of the portable TV. The intercom buzzed. It was Dad.

"Tea's up," he said. "Come on down now. All is forgiven."

It was an old catch phrase of his and melted my heart instantly. Besides, I was hungry. "Okay," I said.

He said, "Did you see the flowers I picked for you? Sorry about the containers. I didn't want to bother Betty for vases." The way he spoke I knew Betty wasn't there.

I said, "They're gorgeous. Where from?"

"The dell. Where we used to go for winter picnics. Remember?"

"Yes." I swallowed. "Yes. Thanks, Dad."

"A pleasure." I could hear him smiling. "Come on down. I want to hear what you and that crazy Nadine have been doing the last three days."

"Okay," I said. Then, because I was feeling better

9

I added, "Okay, Dad. I'm coming. And all *is* forgiven."

I shoved some Charlie toilet water on my neck and ran downstairs, sneaked out the front door and around to the garden, gathered up the forsythia and whipped back the way I'd come. Then I snipped off a head of golden blossom and tucked it behind my ear. I looked in the mirror. Even I could see that I looked like Mum.

Well . . . I wasn't going to write all that down, but if I'm uncovering secrets to find the truth, I suppose it's got to be everyone's secrets. Mine too. There are other people besides Betty who aren't mad about me. I'm one.

Well, that's half the cast. The other half is Mum and her family and . . . Gideon Jones. I'll start on Mum.

On the twelfth of March I was due for a weekend with Mum. The last two times I'd taken Nadine, but then Mum's husband suggested that it was nicer for Mum if I went on my own. "Girls together!" he said heartily. I pointed out that Nadine was a girl too, and he laughed as if I'd made the wittiest joke of the century. "Two's company," he reminded me archly.

I told Nadine that Mum wanted to talk about her

menopause, and Nadine nodded and said she'd skip this weekend if I didn't mind.

"Embarrassed?" I asked, grinning.

"Bored," she corrected. "If my mum describes a hot flash or a palpitation just once more, I shall yawn in her face. Why do women always have to describe their medical symptoms in detail? I mean do I tell you about my ingrown toenails day after day?"

I fell neatly into her trap. "Didn't know you had ingrown toenails."

She grinned and walked off for the Westbury bus. The thing about Nadine Miller is, she can always make me laugh, and that's the best thing you can ask of a best friend. So I went to Mum's alone.

Mum packed up and went off with Alan Forrest when I was three, so we are not exactly easy and familiar with each other. She had kept her figure and her looks over the intervening fourteen years and was modest about it too. "All credit to Helena Rubinstein and Marks and Spencer!" she would say, laughing. "Seriously though, I have to watch it. Alan's profession relies quite heavily on outward appearances."

Alan is an osteopath and treads the delicate path between the National Health reefs and the sleepy shores of private medicine. He is no charlatan; he's got letters after his name from some college in the Midlands. He's a big, handsome man, almost as smart as Mum, and his equipment is all chrome and stainless steel. Their son was ten at this time. His name is

Mark. I didn't know a lot about him because Mum was the exact opposite of Dad and kept him very much in the background when I was around.

She met me off the bus on Weston's long seafront. She was wearing a sage-green woollen frock with her fur coat open down the front and a silk scarf knotted around her throat. Her hair was done in big loose curls all over which emphasized her small face. Her glasses did the rest; they were the size of saucers and tinted blue. There was something about Mum's appearance that made me feel just a touch of sympathy for Betty.

Her smile was wide and she hugged me expertly. I mean her glasses weren't disarranged, her handbag didn't crash into my spine and her makeup wasn't slightly smudged. Yet it was a wholehearted hug.

"Darling. How marvelous. I've been here for the last half hour hoping I'd catch you. We're going to have tea at the Atlantic and go straight on to the theater. I got tickets for the first house. Les McGregor's doing a one-night stand."

I was bowled over. Tea at the Atlantic probably meant prawns and chocolate eclairs and the use of their powder room—an experience all on its own. And Les McGregor was the funniest comedian on television then.

"Gosh. I nearly had Nadine with me," I said unguardedly.

She said simply, "Well, in that case you and Nadine

could have had the tickets. But as it is . . . well, I can come! Treats!" She grinned at me exuberantly and I couldn't help grinning back. Sometimes it was hard to remember she'd walked out on Dad and me.

Nearly the whole thing was a success. As Mum and I never talked about Alan or Mark, Dad or Betty or the twins, our conversational topics were limited, and it was nice to be able to discuss Les McGregor before and after the show. He was terrific in the flesh. Very black and about six foot four and so sexy it was incredible. I loved the big red-velvet cavern of the theater itself and the people and the intermission and everything. Mum bought me a drink at the bar, and she said, "Lemon and lime?" which was my usual, and I nodded and added to the barmaid, "Plenty of vodka with it, please." To my amazement Mum didn't countermand this, so I felt pretty high during the second half and kept thinking how we might meet Les McGregor when we went out, and how I'd sort of stumble against him and he'd say, "Bay-bee!" and roll the whites of his eyes, and we'd live together and make love twenty times a day.

When we really were on the way back, and the awful March wind had dropped and a moon shone on the flat gray sea, I actually told Mum some of this in between giggles. That was when she spoiled it.

We'd got to the house, a three-story Victorian, overlooking Brean Down, with Alan's brass plate glittering in the lamplight, and she laughed with me and said,

"Well . . . now you understand about Alan and me!"

I stopped tittering as if she'd poured a bucket of water over me; I felt hot with embarrassment. Then angry, because why should I feel embarrassed? I looked up at the house. There was a light on in Mark's room, and I knew he was waiting for Mum to go up and say good night. I laughed horribly.

"Sure I understand! You got hot for Alan—sure, I understand that. I'm just surprised you married him. You didn't have to, after all. Not like Betty had to marry Dad."

Still laughing, I walked up the drive, used the key Alan had had specially and magnanimously cut for me and took the stairs two at a time to the room that was always kept for me but was never mine. There was a loose piece of wallpaper just inside the door. I stood with my back pressed hard against the wood while Mum hesitated outside before she went on up to Mark; then I got my nail under the paper and tore it right down to the skirting board.

Saturday she kept away from me, "doing the books." Alan had appointments from eight in the morning till five at night, all women—all in love with him, I expect. I went for a walk on the sands after a kitchen lunch. The wind still kept off, and there was so much gray sky, gray sea and colorless sand it was amazing. I went toward the dunes just before Uphill. The ferry wasn't running, otherwise I could have gone over to Brean itself. I sat on the top of the muddy bank and looked at the narrow channel and tried to think erotic thoughts about Les McGregor.

A voice said, "I thought it was you. Hello."

It was Mark, in the green cap and sweater of the Cub Scouts.

"Hi. I thought you were having an all-day cookout."

"We were. It's finished. We were over there—" He stabbed a finger at the dunes. "Matt Tremoe was sick and I'm not surprised. They fried cowpats."

I had to laugh. "What were they really?"

"Cowpats. Honestly. They used to do that in the Wild West when there was no wood. So Arkala said we'd try it. They stank. I'm surprised you didn't smell them over here."

"Oh, my God." I rolled on my back helplessly and he began to smile.

"What are you doing, Cassie? Why are you here?" he asked at last when I just lay still, grinning.

Nobody calls me Cassie, and I quite liked it coming from him.

"I was just sitting. Thinking. About the show last night. Les McGregor."

"He's great. Did you see him in the *London Palladium Show*?" He squatted by me. "I only like the TV when it makes me laugh."

"Same here. That's why I like him. Nadine. Les McGregor. I like them because they make me laugh." I felt Mark had shown me something significant.

He grinned, pleased I was pleased. "You laugh with Mum sometimes. I've heard you."

16

"Yes. Sometimes."

"And you laughed just now about the cowpats."

"I adore cowpats!"

He hooted, understanding that I meant I liked him. Then he said, "Let's *do* something! What can we do? It's been a horrible Saturday. Can't we do something special?"

I looked all around for inspiration, not wanting to let down my half brother. There was the sky right down to the sea. Dunes one side, the mighty head of Brean in front, divided from us by the trickle of brown water.

"Explore?" I asked, because that's about all you can do with space.

He leaned forward, frowning, chewing his top lip, considering the terrain with all his might.

"We could make a raft. Get over the river. That's the first obstacle."

I leaped up. "Right. Wood. Planks. An old door. Anything."

We were galvanized into action. Almost immediately I found a big flat piece of wood with a message painted on it: DANGER. SINKING SANDS. It hadn't sunk. Mark came up with a tangle of fishing net. He said, "If we collect all the Coke cans we can find, we might be able to fix them onto that notice board thing with this net."

"They'll have holes in the top," I reminded him.

He shrugged impatiently. "We must bung them up with mud."

Well, there's enough mud on Weston beach to bung up a million Coke cans, and that's about how many cans we bunged up. It kept us busy and laughing for the next hour. It also made us very dirty.

We bundled the bunged-up cans into the net and put the board on top, then we carried the lot down to the ferry rope that straddled the estuary and chucked it on to the water.

"Bleedin' 'ell," Mark marveled, relishing the oaths deliciously. "It's floating!"

"Don't swear. All aboard for a trip round the bay."

It was tricky getting onto the rocking contraption, and we became wet as well as dirty—wetter still when we hauled ourselves over on the waterlogged rope.

"Next obstacle!" Mark yelled, brandishing his arm at the field leading up to the headland; we charged across it as if we were an attacking army. It warmed us up. We were panting and hot when we reached the top and looked down on a different sea spreading southwest toward America itself.

"The Atlantic," I said, awed.

Mark nodded. "Yes. That's a good name for it. We'll call it the Atlantic."

We walked along the spine of the headland, which brooded quietly over the huge length of Berrow Sands and the Somerset Levels, until we came to a bit of sandy cliff without rock or grass, obviously used as a chute in the summer.

"We came here before. D'you remember?" I sat down. The sand was powder-fine and bright red.

"Alan . . . your father slid down on the picnic tray with you in front. He wanted me to have a go, but I wouldn't."

But Mark couldn't remember; he'd been about four. I'd been eleven and still able to hate Mum and Alan wholeheartedly. It was B.B. That meant Before Betty.

He sat by me. "Do we need a tray?" He pushed himself off and coasted down on his back shrieking with joy. When he stood up at the bottom, his green Cub jersey was torn and the shirt underneath bright red.

I yelled, "Don't go away!" I launched myself off and felt the studs of my jeans scoring a set of parallel lines in the soft sand as I slid gracefully, almost sedately, to the foot of the cliff. Mark was hysterical with excitement. We climbed up and did it again. Then headfirst, then prone. Then backward.

It was getting dark. We began to trudge back to the river and our raft. We were tired but happy. I couldn't remember when I'd been so simply and completely happy. Then we discovered that the raft had gone.

Mark said, "Cheer up. We can go to one of those houses. Ask them to ring Mum, and she'll come and fetch us in the car."

It's nearly ten miles back to Weston by road.

"She'll blame me. You're filthy. Oh damn! Dammitall! Why didn't I *think*!"

Mark sounded a bit scared. "Nothing is wrong, Cassie. We've had fun. That's all."

"Oh, God! You don't understand."

His voice was very small. "Mustn't I play with you, Cassie?"

I didn't look at him. Not that I could have seen him by that time—it was the darkest damned night I've ever not seen in. But he wasn't daft, obviously; he'd noticed that Mum kept us apart.

I said, "Don't be stupid. Why on earth shouldn't you play with me? I haven't got mumps or anything, have I?"

He laughed, reassured. "No. More like scarlet fever. You're covered in that sand stuff."

"Oh, Lord . . ." I considered swimming across using the rope to guide me, but Mark couldn't have done it. In the end we did what he'd suggested and trudged back up the fields to the nearest cottage. It wasn't that easy. There were two fences and what felt like a field of cabbages; the fences were strung with barbed wire and the cabbages had characters like something out of *The Day of the Triffids*. The woman who opened the door to us was frightened at first; she wouldn't let us past her porch, so we gave her the Forrest number and waited while she dialed.

"Mrs. Forrest is that? I've got your children here. No, nothing to worry about, they say, but it looks to me as if they've been in some kind of accident or something. Not injured exactly, no . . . but they're bleeding. Yes, both of them. Yes, the boy as well. Not fit to get up to the road for the bus, I wouldn't think. . . . You know the way? There's a track up to the house, but no light." She came back to us. "Your mam's coming. Your dad's gone out for the evening. Sounds lucky to me." She shoved at a tea chest with her toe. "Here, sit on this and I'll get you some cocoa. You could come in, only I've cleaned through."

I said nothing, did nothing, but Mark perched on the tea chest and smiled at her. "That's quite all right. Thank you for the cocoa."

I looked at him, amazed at his charm. Did it come from Mum or Alan? It had warmed me all afternoon, I realized now. I could almost dislike him for it. And I could understand why Mum loved him and protected him from me.

She arrived too quickly for safety; and she'd remembered to take one of the boxes of Lindt chocolates the lady patients brought for Alan. She presented it to our unwilling hostess with warm thanks.

It wasn't until we'd got out of the car and she'd posted Mark to the bathroom with a rueful laugh that she showed me her real feelings.

"Was it your latest idea of revenge?" she said, small nostrils distended, mouth thin. "I suppose I should be grateful you didn't actually push him into the water! There seems to be nothing you won't do in your campaign!"

"Campaign?" I felt sluggish and stupid. "I don't know what you mean. Mark found me on the beach and wanted to do something different, and—"

"My God, Cass! Ever since you came here first—

21

long before Mark was born—you tried to wreck my marriage. Don't deny it! You were seven years old then, now you're seventeen. Your methods are more subtle, I'll give you that. I suppose Dad's told you I was in a mental hospital, did he? And you think you can put me back there! Is that it?"

I stared at her. The words didn't go in . . . then. I was so appalled at the dislike on her face, I could register nothing else.

She was practically hissing. "I'm telling you now, Cass . . . you won't send me out of my mind a second time! I'd kill myself first! Do you hear me? Do you understand?"

I went on staring. She waited for an answer. At last I said, "Yes."

And went upstairs.

3

I suppose that was the first secret. It wasn't much of one really. Lots of people have nervous breakdowns these days and spend a month or two in psychiatric hospitals. But no one had told me that it had happened to Mum. Why should they, after all? But it made me feel . . . funny. I didn't ask Dad about it and I didn't tell Nadine.

Anyway, next things next. Enter Gideon Jones.

It was Monday, lunchtime. Raining, of course. We were in a coffee shop sitting at the counter in front of plate-glass mirrors. We had a perfect view of three apprentices from the engineering school who were sitting in the corner trying not to notice us. This must have been difficult, because not only had Nadine streaked her hair over the weekend but she kept making ghastly faces in the mirror at them.

She was in the middle of a fairly boring account of her weekend.

"It was June Parry put me up to doing my hair. D'you like it?" Another grimace and the apprentices looked quickly down into their coffee cups. "It didn't quite work. I must get another bottle and . . . Anyway, where did I get to? Parry and me went to the Essoldo, and she said wouldn't it be great if we could go to Sweden with the boys, and I said—"

"What was the film?"

"Film? Oh, at the Essoldo. I forget. Anyway, I said I'd forge a letter from Mrs. Prior to old Tyson suggesting it."

"Suggesting what?"

She exploded suddenly. "Christ, Cass! You haven't listened to a blasted word I've said, have you?" She paused, stuck her tongue out at the mirror and turned to face me. "Look. The apprentices are going to visit the Volvo works at Easter. Sweden. Right? What better experience could the secretarial school have than going with them and taking notes of what happens!"

I said sourly, "I can just imagine what would happen if June Parry is allowed to run amok with the engineering apprentices."

"So can I," Nadine agreed with relish.

"And June Parry put you up to forging a letter to the head of the engineering school, old Tyson himself?"

"You don't like June Parry."

"She's a bad influence on you," I said piously. "You're going to be in big trouble, and she'll sit back and laugh."

"You're so blasted cautious these days, Cass Durston! You seem to have overlooked that life is for living! And you've got to go out and grab it when you can and how you can!"

"Like June Parry?" I swiveled my stool, got the full attention of the three in the corner and pouted lasciviously at them. Two of them grinned appreciatively; the other one frowned. He had ginger hair and a mass of orange freckles and very pale blue eyes. It gave him no right whatsoever to disapprove of me, pouting or unpouting. I turned back to Nadine. "See what I mean?"

She choked with laughter. "Still, it would be great if we could get Mrs. Prior to take us to Sweden with that lot. Admit it."

I glanced quickly in the mirror and met those pale-blue, critical eyes. But I wasn't going to admit a thing.

I said pleasantly, "How are the ingrown toenails, Nadine?"

We were giggling as usual when we left. The apprentices were staring with all their eyes. I stopped by the door and blew them a kiss. Well . . . life is for living.

We also had Mrs. Prior for human studies. That afternoon six of us went in a minibus to an adult training center in Weston. I peered through the low windows wondering whether I might see Mark, though I knew he'd be at school. Then I stopped peering, lest I see Mum.

Nadine said persuasively, "Sweden is so different, Mrs. Prior. Most of us have been to France and places. Sweden is something else."

"My dear child, I can't speak Swedish, can you?"

"No. But Mr. Tyson can."

"Mr. Tyson? The engineering school?" She looked over her shoulder, suspicion lengthening her nice round face.

I rushed to Nadine's aid. "A couple of the girls have boyfriends in the engineering school, Mrs. Prior. They found out that Mr. Tyson is taking a group to the Volvo works."

Mrs. Prior said, "I see." Her gaze slid across to me. She thought I was a "nice girl" because I lived on a farm. And she wanted to believe us. She called us "her girls."

We parked outside another Victorian building. She said slowly, "As a matter of fact, Mr. Tyson has suggested something about the trip. I must have a word with him."

We all got out and I gave Nadine my told-you-so look. Then we went to the back of the house, where there was a sort of shed-*cum*-workshop. Tables were everywhere and each table had its quota of mongoloid workers. A green-coated woman welcomed us and told us everyone thought it was just lovely that we had come and we were just in time for a cup of tea, which Winnie and Harold were going to make because it was their turn. Harold and Winnie stood up, full of self-importance. Harold was elderly and stooped; Winnie looked younger, with an enormously jutting bottom lip, bulging forehead and sparse black hair. Nadine and I looked at each other again but without smiles.

After a bit of maneuvering, we found ourselves distributed among the tables, obviously expected to be full of admiration for the way that the manufacturer's tags were being attached with a sort of nylon stapler to plastic bags. It was awful. Winnie brought a cup of tea to me, carrying it as if it were the Holy Grail, mouth open, tongue out, eyes crossed with concentration. She and the other four at my table watched me sample it.

"Delicious," I lied.

That was a mistake. They were over the moon; Winnie had to sit on my lap and stroke my hair. She had terrific B.O. Nadine caught my eye again, and again we didn't smile.

Afterward she said, "Made me think of that day at the hypermarket."

"No wonder the ape woman went mad with us for mucking about," I agreed gloomily.

June Parry thought it was a case for euthanasia. Mrs. Prior said, "What are your criteria for being permitted to live, then, June?"

Parry flushed. "Well . . . if you can't give anything . . . I mean *contribute* . . . to society, then surely . . ." She got under way, quoting a book or TV program by the sound of it.

Mrs. Prior made a noise that sounded like "shit" but obviously couldn't have been. She said, "I suppose it depends on what you call society. But those people in there contribute. Everyone contributes. Make no mistake about that."

Parry went rabbiting on, but I didn't hear the rest. Someone else had arrived at the gate of the center and was being vociferously welcomed by Winnie and Harold. I peered, intrigued. It was the lavender-and-pound-note-scented lady from the hypermarket who had been landed with the chewed Double Gloucester cheese. She put her arms right round Winnie and did not flinch from Harold's wet kiss. They all went in together.

There were a lot of us in the coffee shop after college. The apprentices were overwhelmed and pretended not to know what we were talking about, so that the explanations would take half an hour instead of ten minutes.

June Parry rolled her eyes with exasperation, thrust out the front of her T-shirt and began for the third time, this time giving credit where credit was due.

"Nadine wrote this letter supposed to be—"

"Nadine?" The pale-blue-eyed one looked at me questioningly.

I said, "I'm Cass. She's Nadine."

Parry said impatiently, "Never mind the formal introductions. Our woman, Mrs. Prior, is going to have a word with your Mr. Tyson about this letter. Can you cover for us?"

Pale eyes said, "You want to come to Sweden with us?"

He was asking me, but I said nothing.

Parry said, "Well, it's better than staying at home, I suppose."

One of the other boys said, "I'm all for it. Gidd, you can fix Tyson, can't you?"

I yelped, "*Gidd*?"

Pale eyes said levelly, "Gideon. Gideon Jones." He stared at me unsmilingly. "Do *you* want to come to Sweden with us?"

I couldn't hold his stare. I shrugged. "Don't know," I said brilliantly.

Nadine said, "Of course she does. It was her idea in the first place."

For some unaccountable reason I was furious. "It was not!"

But Gideon Jones said, "Okay then. I'll fix Tyson."

Nadine and I were wide-eyed. We did not doubt he'd be able to do it.

Nadine said, "He fancies you. He really does."

I fancied him too. My pelvis tingled and my thighs shook.

Nadine said, "If . . . when we get to this place in Sweden . . . if . . . when . . . he asks you . . . will you?"

"Will I what?"

"*You* know! Will you?"

I said piously, "I'm saving myself for Les McGregor, actually."

Nadine filled her cheeks with air and exploded it. "Oh, shut up!"

We giggled and started fantasizing. I thought, Well, why not? I'm not allowed anywhere near Jennifer, Jacqueline or Mark. Mum hates me and Dad is only keen at times. If Gideon Jones wants that . . . why not?

It rained that weekend, which meant Dad cut down on the outside work, Betty couldn't take the twins for a walk and I stayed in too. Sustained claustrophobia. It also meant that I couldn't detach Dad from the others long enough to ask him about the cash for Sweden.

I hung about in the kitchen most of Sunday, forcing Betty to let me peel the potatoes for lunch and wash up afterward. Dad spread the paper all over the table and tried to ignore the twins. I noticed Betty gulping an aspirin with her coffee, so I got down on the floor and made a complicated structure of bricks for the kids. Betty didn't like it, but she sat watching us helplessly, looking as if she had a champion migraine. I actually felt sorry for her.

At four o'clock Dad got himself out of the chair with difficulty and announced he'd better start the evening milk. Betty watched the paper fall off the table and didn't leap forward when I picked it up and folded it.

I said, "I'll walk over to the shed with you, Dad. Could do with some fresh air."

Jennifer began to cry and put her arms round my leg.

"Stay with the kids," Dad said carelessly. "Make some tea."

Betty jumped up, laughing. "I'll make the tea, Cass." She tore Jennifer off my leg and kept laughing through Jen's screams. "You go on with your father, dear."

I wished I didn't believe that she wanted to get rid of me. She was already filling the kettle with one hand; Jack was banging Dad's chair up and down. I followed Dad into the lobby and put on my boots. We trooped outside into the mud. In spite of the thick walls of the farmhouse, the racket from inside was plain and clear.

"Bloody kids!" Dad said. But he said it humorously.

The rain had released a dozen smells of spring and summer from the winter earth. From the door of the sheds I looked up at our shoulder of Mendip, hunched into the gray sky, and could almost feel it stir from its hibernation. The brook that ran through our winter picnic place was gushing along the bottom of the pasture like a river, and I could see some yellow dots on its south bank that were probably primroses. The milking machine hummed behind me. I thought of a word: fecund. I swallowed and went into the darkness of the sheds.

"Dad. I wanted to ask you something."

His eyes glinted amusement. "Thought so. That's why you've been so damned helpful all weekend. Crafty little madam."

"Seriously, Dad. There's a trip from college. It will cost. But it should be"—I swallowed again—"quite an experience."

He checked the dials, turned a switch, stepped up to one of the cows and took off the tubes.

"Where to?"

"Sweden."

His head came up. "Sweden? Good God, girl. I thought you were training to be some sort of secretary?"

"That's where they all come from, Dad. Cool. Efficient. You remember Greta Garbo? Ingrid Bergman?"

"Sex. That's all I know about Sweden. Free sex."

"You would." It was hot in the sheds. I went to the door and spoke over my shoulder. "Not my choice. Mrs. Prior's. Well, what about it?"

There was a long and unusual silence. It hadn't occurred to me that Dad wouldn't fork out for me to go. I glanced back at him.

He joined me. "Listen, Cass." He sounded uncomfortable. "How keen are you?"

"Not that keen."

"Is that crazy Nadine going?"

"Yes."

"Damn." He stared with me at the dark shape of Mendip. "Damn."

I knew that meant no. I said, "That doesn't mean *I* want to go. Forget it, Dad."

"It's just that money's tight right now, honey. I'll see what I can do, though. Talk to your mother."

"No. Don't do that. It doesn't matter. Honestly."

"They're rolling, Cass. And she likes to feel—"

"Dad, I don't want you to ask Mother."

"Only, just at the moment it's rather difficult for me to—"

"Dad, it's *okay*. Really."

"You see, Betty's expecting again, and if she does what she did last time and produces more than one . . ." He laughed as if it were a family joke and I was in on it.

I opened my mouth incredulously, then closed it. Betty, white-faced and at the aspirin. Betty, permitting me to help her for once.

I said, "Congratulations, Dad."

I sloshed back to the house, left my boots in the entryway again and went upstairs. I lay on my bed and thought about Dad and Betty. Then I thought about Les McGregor. Then I thought about Gideon Jones.

With a sob I resorted to masturbation.

I didn't tell Nadine that the Swedish trip was off for me. I don't know why. I like to think I was being unselfish; Nadine herself would probably have backed down if she had known I wasn't going. But it was more likely I was being a martyr. It seemed the only role left to play just then.

It went on raining for the rest of March. I didn't see Mum. Nadine and I spent time together on weekends. I realized that I was going to survive Dad's perfidy a second time, but that didn't give me a lot of kicks. I felt more in the way than ever at the farm, and Betty looked like death warmed up.

April the first dawned. All Fools' Day. I wiped a space in the condensation of my window and looked through. It actually wasn't raining, and the sun was leaning casually on top of Mendip as if it had all day in which to shine. There was a small scratchy sound below, and I pressed my nose to the glass and looked down. In the flower bed below Betty was picking primroses. She had a small, tight nosegay in her left hand, and with her right she followed a stalk down to its base and gently nicked it off. She worked gently and lovingly.

I went downstairs just as the phone started to ring.

"Hello. Is that Mendip four two eight nine?"

"Yeah." Dad was out, Betty was out, the twins still asleep. I didn't have to be polite.

"Is that you, Cass?"

"Yes." I straightened, surprised. Nadine was the only one who phoned me. This was male, solid and male. It was Alan.

"Hi, Cass. It's Alan. I hoped I would catch you before you whipped off to college. How's things?"

"Okay." I felt a pang of anxiety. "Is anything wrong, Alan?"

"Not a thing. Everything's fine. Dandy. I just wanted a word between ourselves. Private." I waited. He said, "Look, Cass. A bit awkward for me, old girl, but . . . about this trip to Sweden—"

"It's off," I interrupted swiftly. I could kill Dad and his big mouth at times.

There was a pause; then he said with a perspicacity

I wouldn't have believed possible, "I don't believe you, Cass. Stop being proud. This is nothing to do with your mother at all. I want you to go on that trip—enjoy yourself. Call it next year's birthday and Christmas present combined. I shall put a check in the post this morning—I don't want any thank-you notes—just tell me how much."

I stared along the length of the hall. A hobbyhorse was draped with Dad's scarf and balaclava, two of Jenny's building bricks were just inside the front door. Betty did her best, but she was up against a lot of opposition. I thought of the hall where Alan was now standing. Flowers, whatever time of the year, the long cheval mirror, the sunshine from Brean Head shining through the colored glass of the front door.

I said, "It's marvelous of you, Alan. Honestly. But I was serious. The trip is off. It was a mixed group and probably they thought it was safer to let the boys go on their own."

He was nonplussed—I felt it over the wire. I rushed on again, "Thanks for the offer, though. I'll bear it in mind next time I need a fur coat. Or another car." It was getting heavy. I forced a laugh. "Listen, Alan. I have to go. Breakfast."

I put the phone down very carefully lest he feel I was cutting him off; then I stared at the hobbyhorse wondering whether I'd cut off my nose to spite my face. But I couldn't take charity from Mum's husband, could I?

Betty came in and put the primroses into an eggcup

and had some shredded wheat with me. She usually fetched the twins when we were threatened with being alone together, so I ought to have guessed that the next funny thing was due to happen. Sure enough, it did.

She said, "I suppose your father has told you I'm pregnant again."

A piece of shredded wheat got in my throat, but I refused to cough and look as if I were choking with emotion. I grunted.

She said, "I don't feel well, Cass. I have to get away for a bit. Have a rest. Could you . . . would you . . . cope here?"

I couldn't believe my ears.

"Where will you go?"

"My mother's. In Weymouth. She's been after me for ages to go for a holiday. She'd like you to go too, Cass. She always asks after you. Perhaps one day . . ."

I ignored that. It was tricky enough living with Betty without meeting her family. I knew her mother was a widow and ran a boardinghouse in Weymouth, so she could never find the time to visit us. Thank goodness.

I said, "Not much of a break for you, really. Keeping the twins away from the guests."

"Actually, with Easter coming up, Mummy has got a full house. I wondered . . ." She was watching me now, her blue eyes bulbous with entreaty. "Cass, I know it's a lot to ask—"

I could have helped her out. I didn't. It seemed strange to think Betty had a "Mummy."

She stumbled on hopelessly. "They adore you, Cass. And you're more efficient than me. I wouldn't leave till you start your Easter vacation, and I'd be back in good time for the summer term."

I nearly said: Alan's paying for me to go to Sweden. But then she'd insist I take up his offer and I couldn't be a martyr.

I shrugged instead. "Okay. If you think I can cope, I'll do it. You'll have to leave me instructions. Food and so forth." I took my cereal dish to the sink so that I wouldn't have to watch her red face as she thanked me. Then she got up and fetched the eggcup of primroses. "Put these in your room, Cass. I know you like flowers, and they smell so sweet. I picked them for you."

I took them. I thought of her out there this morning picking them with all that tenderness. The piece of shredded wheat tickled my throat again and I choked at last.

As if it had been carefully timetabled, Mrs. Prior announced that morning that the trip to Sweden was on and we must arrange our own passports and bring a check the next day as a nonrefundable deposit. Nadine was over the moon.

"It's all my doing. You realize that?" she asked, raking out her streaked hair with spread fingers. "Let's go to the coffee shop at lunchtime and see if Gideon Jones wants congratulating."

The thought of Gideon Jones made me regret my martyrdom, and when we got to the coffee shop and saw him sitting there with his expressionless face managing to register censoriousness, I was conscious of pelvis and thighs again. Also a tight sensation inside my chest cavity that had nothing to do with sex and was just plain regret.

He didn't rise to Nadine's rallying, and she soon gave up and turned to his friend, who was more responsive.

"How did he do it?" she asked, jerking her head at Gideon.

He grinned. "Probably told Tyson the naked truth. A great one for the naked truth is Gidd."

They sparred over that, the innuendos sprouting thick and fast. Gideon said, "How many of you are coming?"

Nadine pouted. "A dozen probably. Cass and me, of course. June Parry. Sofie Marks. About a dozen."

The other boy started on at her again: Couldn't she add up? His name was Maurice Latham. Nadine called him Morrie.

Under cover of their racket Gideon said, "Cass. Is that short for Cassandra?"

"No. Just Catherine."

"You don't have much to say, Catherine."

"I have a lot to think about. That could be it."

"Could be." He smiled. "When we're in Sweden, how about telling me some of your thoughts?"

I shrugged, wanting to tell him I wouldn't be there, not able to because I hadn't told Nadine.

"Won't be much time for that, I shouldn't think."

His smile died and his pale eyes were intent. "We'll make time."

I felt weak and all-powerful at the same time. I said, "We'll see. My thoughts are fairly private actually. I don't go much for this truth-and-consequences game."

He glanced at Nadine and Maurice, wrangling acerbically. Then he treated me to his lovely smile again and said, "I'm not much good at the other kind of games, Catherine. Sorry."

I think it was then that I loved him. Warmth flooded my chest cavity and I wanted to laugh and say thank you for being bright and honest and inviting me to be honest too.

But I'm not honest.

I smiled very deliberately. "You should learn," I said.

He looked disappointed for a minute. Then he said very slowly, "Okay. If that's the way you want it. I'll try."

It was as if we'd been arm wrestling and I'd won. Or he'd surrendered. Either way I should have felt triumph. But I didn't. There was a sweetness in Gideon Jones that did not show through the gingerness and the freckles. But it was there. And it was his sweetness that had won.

We couldn't actually pay our deposits the next day because it was Saturday. Which gave me the weekend to work out how I was going to break the news of

40

my betrayal to Nadine—because of course she'd look on my backing down from the Swedish trip as a betrayal.

Anyway, she phoned just at coffee time when Dad was eating his late breakfast in stony silence, Betty was near tears and I was being allowed to dress the twins and take them for a walk.

"Hey," Nadine said. "Your stepfather just phoned."

"My—?" I never thought of Alan as a stepfather. "What the hell for?"

Jennifer seized the handle of her hobbyhorse and shoved it hard against the stairs. She did it again. And again.

"To ask me how much the trip is costing. He's putting a check in the post for you. What's that noise? Is the farm falling down?"

"Yes." I leaned out and restrained Jennifer and she swung the horse round into my shins. I doubled up. "I wish you hadn't told him how much."

"Why? I thought it was lovely of him to ask me. So that it it would be a surprise for you."

"Oh, sure. But something's come up." I removed the handle of the horse from Jenny's clutching fingers.

"What?" queried Nadine.

"I can't talk now. Tell you Monday."

"What's going on? What are you doing?" This last as Jenny began to scream.

"Getting the twins ready for a walk. See you."

"But Betty never lets you within a mile of them, you said. You said she—"

"Betty's not well. Tell you Monday."

I put the phone down quickly before Betty could erupt from the kitchen. Then I placed the horse on the floor and swung Jenny onto its back. She shut up. I got Jack's parka and shoved her into it. Red plastic boots. My own parka and boots.

"See you in an hour!" I called into the kitchen.

I enjoyed being out with those small girls. When I could stop thinking of them as belonging to Betty and Dad, they were okay. Noisy, aggressive, full of awe at things like worms and cobwebs and muddy puddles, they were a full-time job. I took them to our winter picnic place, where the forsythia was in massed bloom and frog spawn floated in clumps among the weeds. We got some flat stones and made a harbor to stop the spawn going off with the current, and I promised we'd come back soon with jars and collect some. Then we clambered to a place where there was a view of Blagdon Lake, and we played cave bears till it was time to go back for our midday dinner. It was marvelous to see the sun after so much rain. We got hot and took off our parkas and slung them over our shoulders. We trudged back along the road singing "The Happy Wanderer." They kept perfect time, and they frowned as they sang and kept reshouldering their slippery coats and taking it all very seriously. I was glad they had each other.

The check came before I left Monday morning. Betty was still in bed and Dad was outside. I looked at it. There was no note or anything. Just "Pay Miss

Catherine Durston eighty-four pounds only" and signed Alan B. Forrest. The temptation was awful. I had only to show it to Betty and she'd cancel her holiday instantly. Like Dad had said, Alan was rolling in money. It was nothing to him. Like keeping a special room for me in his house and having a front-door key cut.

I went over to the stove and took off the hot plate and dropped in the check. It would have been more dramatic to let it burn slowly between my fingers. At least I didn't do that.

Nadine said, "I don't *get* it! Why should you do anything for *her*? She seduced your Dad so that he'd have to marry her, and now she's done it again just so that she can have a blasted holiday with an unpaid nursemaid to look after her kids!"

"It's not like that," I said wearily, because we'd been going over and over it for the past half hour. "She's not well! She needs to get away for a bit. And I'd decided not to take Alan's money anyway."

"It doesn't make sense." Nadine stopped raging and stared at me, genuinely puzzled. Then she played her trump card. "What about Gideon Jones?"

"You can have him," I said lightly.

"He fancies you."

I returned her look.

"Okay. I admit that hurts. And if it gives you any satisfaction, I also admit that if he'd asked me, I would have. So, now you know."

She said, "Oh, *Cass* . . ."

I thought I might cry. To hell with Gideon Jones—
I was going to miss Nadine Miller like a nice familiar
stitch in the side. She reminded me always that life
was for running, never walking sedately.

I said, "Oh, shut up. Just enjoy yourself. And come
back and tell me everything. D'you hear? I want to
know every last little thing!"

She wiped her nose inelegantly on her wrist.
"You . . . you blasted Judas!" she said.

5

The attraction of being a martyr soon lost its allure. The day they left I kept checking the time. Nine o'clock they were meeting at the bus station. Eleven-thirty they were due at Newhaven. Twelve-thirty lunch was served aboard the *Hans Lufsven* and at one o'clock there'd be a lot of chain rattling and shouting as they cast off. It was awful.

Then it was April 15 and Betty left for Weymouth. Suddenly, within an hour of her departure, I was too busy to worry about missing anything or anywhere. Jack wanted the pot, Jenny was making pastry and got it all over the chair, the dog hadn't been fed and

I couldn't find the can opener for his food. April 16 was a repeat performance varied by Jenny throwing her stewed apple at Dad. April 17 I took them for a walk in the afternoon, they waded in the harbor we'd made, the water came over the tops of their boots and by the evening they were snuffling and sneezing and complaining of the cold.

That night Jenny's yells sent me scurrying along the landing to the nursery. Jack had been sick all over her cot.

"Want Mummy," she whimpered.

It was awful. Her blond hair was dry and light and stuck up at the back like a duck's tail. She knuckled her eyes. I knew how she felt. Dimly, so dimly that it seemed like a dream, I remembered wanting Mum. But then, I'd had Dad.

I whispered, "Shall I fetch Daddy?"

They said nothing. Betty had drilled into them that Daddy must have his sleep because he had to be up early to milk the cows.

I said hesitantly, "Will you come and sleep with me then?"

Jack took her hands out of her eyes and blinked. Jenny extricated herself from her bedclothes and stood up. I changed Jack's nightie and carried her down the landing and Jenny followed.

The snag was I didn't get a lot of sleep for the rest of the night, and instead of staying in bed while I cleaned up for an hour, they came with me. I found I was worried about them, and since I wanted the doctor to come, I had to phone the Health Center before nine. Dad didn't come in before then, so I did it off my own bat.

"Are the children running a temperature?" asked the receptionist.

"I don't know. One of them was sick in the night."

"But they're not feverish? They're awake?"

"Oh, yes. They're playing as usual. But—"

"Are you sure you can't bring them down to the Center? The doctor has a lot of calls to make—"

My voice rose to a wail. "I dare not take them out again! I think they caught chills yesterday when they got wet. Please ask the doctor to come—please."

"Very well, dear. Try to keep calm. Liquids only. Save the bowel movements for the doctor to examine."

"Oh, my God!" Both girls had had bacon sandwiches already, and I'd disposed of the potty contents.

"*Keep calm*," reiterated the heartless receptionist.

Dad said, "Why on earth didn't you call me? I could have told you there was nothing wrong with them. My God, I got you through mumps and measles—"

"We didn't want to wake you. Jack wasn't sick again otherwise—"

"Did you see what she ate at teatime yesterday? I'm not surprised she was sick."

"Yes, but . . . Dad, I'm sorry, I haven't looked after them properly. They got soaked yesterday. And I gave them ice cream on cold tummies—"

"You sound like Betty."

I wanted to cry. "They asked for her. In the night."

Suddenly he understood. I daresay he had had to cope with me asking for Mum. He said, "D'you want me to ring her at Weymouth? Ask her to come back?"

I did start to cry then. I'd wanted Betty to stay away forever. Jack started to cry too. I sobbed, "If they want her . . ."

Dad hoisted Jack into the air. "Why you cry?" he demanded like Tarzan.

Her mouth upended itself and she chuckled.

"See?" He put her down. "She was crying because you were crying." He shook his head slowly at me. "They love you, you idiot. You're their big sister."

I was stuck. I wanted to be in Sweden. I wanted to be here. I wanted Betty to stay away. I wanted her back. I didn't know what the hell I did want. Except bed. I was so tired. . . .

The doctor said there was nothing wrong with them and why didn't we all have a nap right now.

"The sheets are full of sick," I told him.

"Ah. Got sleeping bags?"

"Yes."

"Put them in sleeping bags; they'll think it's a treat."

I did that. I admit I felt better; stronger. I was able to do the washing and cook some French fries for tea. On the other hand, life was still fairly savorless.

Dad said tactfully, "Time of the month, chick?"

"Pre-men tension?" I asked, giving him a look. "No,

Dad. Nothing like that. Just a touch of clear vision for once. I'm not nice."

"Listen, chick," Dad said earnestly. "You're nice. You're lovely. Isn't she, kids?"

He was sitting with the twins on his lap and they were supposedly watching *Doctor Who.* Contentment was like a visible bubble enclosing all three of them. They didn't answer him, naturally, and he grinned up at me.

"You are anyway. Beautiful too. Look, why don't you catch the bus and go down to Weston? Have a coffee with Mum. Walk along the prom. Catch the ten-thirty back. I'll put the kids to bed."

"No thanks. No, I'll have an early night myself."

He didn't press it. When he took Jenny and Jack upstairs, I went outside the back door and stood very still gazing up at our hills lit by the evening sun. It was a trick I'd perfected Before Betty when I was missing Mum. I'd stand there and pretend I was a bird and I could see everything from above. I'd fly up Burrington Coombe and along the old Wells road, taking in Priddy and maybe Ebor Gorge and Wookey; then sweep over the moat and the cathedral and the tiny ancient city and on to Glastonbury with its tor and ruins and Holy Thorn, then circle back home over the lakes. Sometimes it worked. I'd feel at once calm, omnipotent and part of my little piece of Earth. But then . . . I'd been a kid. It didn't work anymore. The Mendips were beautiful but they refused to accept me. I shivered.

The phone began to ring. Pips sounded in my ear, then a coin dropped and a voice said, "May I speak to Miss Catherine Durston, please."

I looked in startled amazement at the hobbyhorse.

"It's not . . . it can't be. You're supposed to be in Sweden! My God, what has happened?"

"How did you know it was me?"

How could it be anyone else with that curious, light voice?

"No one else calls me Catherine. It *is* you?"

"Yes. It's me."

It was him. Gideon Jones. I forgot the lonely Mendips and the loneliness. My heart thudded throughout my body, even in my toes.

"What are you *doing*? What has *happened*?"

"I didn't go, of course."

"Why?"

"You weren't going."

"But your deposit—"

"They let me have it back. It wouldn't have mattered. It was my own money."

"My God. I can't believe it. You're mad."

"I don't think so." He paused, then said, "I haven't got any more change. I'm at Weston. There's a fair. Can you come?"

"Yes."

"I've got my motorbike. D'you want me to pick you up?"

"No. There's a bus. My God, you're mad."

"What time does the bus get in?"

"Just before eight."

"I'll be at the bus station. Don't miss it."

The pips began. "I won't. My God. You're mad."

I stared at the humming phone and wondered whether I'd dreamed it and knew I had not. He'd been the one to organize the Swedish trip; he'd set it up somehow. He'd been going. And when he heard I wasn't . . . I banged the receiver down and went to the mirror. My hair was flat and I looked ghastly. I found a brush and my makeup and went to work.

Dad called, "What was all that about? Where are you off to?"

"Weston." It would take too long to explain. "Just like you suggested," I said.

He assumed it had been Mum on the phone. I hadn't said it was, though.

I'd like to skip the next bit. I really would. But if I did, then what happened after wouldn't really make sense. I mean, if Gideon and I hadn't started off on the wrong foot, maybe he wouldn't have tried so hard to get on the right foot later. Maybe he wouldn't have helped me to find out the secret places of the stairs.

I don't know.

But somehow, there's no way out of it. Sometime, somehow, I've got to learn how to be honest.

So there I was, done up to the nines, sitting on the Weston bus, going to meet a bloke who'd given up quite a lot just to be with me. It was enough to go to anyone's head, wasn't it?

6

He was waiting at the bus station, his ginger hair and freckles and pale, clear eyes curiously bright above his motorbike leathers. He looked beautiful.

The cavernous station smelled of gas and exhaust fumes and was garish with fluorescent tubes. We walked over rainbow-shot oil slicks and onto the blowing promenade and looked at each other with total awareness. Everything else, the whole universe, but especially Weston Prom with its gritty wind and a kid on a skateboard and the hot-dog stands and the cloudy tented sky above, all of it existed for us. We were the reason it had been created. Everything that had happened before in world history, everything that would happen in the future, had happened for this moment and would be the direct result of this moment.

We might have stood there forever if it hadn't been for the donkeys. It was almost Easter and they'd been out all day on the sands trekking back and forth, heads down, eyes dreaming and secretive. Now they were going home, hay still clinging to their mouths, their long lashes drooping. They literally pushed between us, driven by a grinning boy in denims and Stetson. Their dusty, donkey smell was homely and simple. I looked across their tatty gray backs and met Gideon's eyes again, and we began to laugh.

When they'd gone, we joined up quite naturally. His arm went over my shoulders, mine went round his waist, and we drifted along toward Locking Road and the derelict area where the Sunday market and the football ground huddled behind the railway station. The fair was switched on in every sense of the word: lights, sound, movement, smell. We moved into its aura automatically; it claimed us, drew us in and swallowed us whole. We pulsated with it.

The burly Gypsy in charge of the rifle range saw us coming through the cacophony and leaned out to grab Gideon's shoulder.

"Come on now, lad—show 'er what y'r made of. Eh?" He brandished a shining gun. "Show 'er what you can do when you got the right kind of equipment!" He gave a throaty chuckle at his own innuendo and I felt a sort of shock go through Gideon's frame. He released me so that we could stare at each other again. This time our awareness went one degree further. Or back. Which was it? Before, we'd known—we'd been totally conscious of—our oneness. Now, we recognized our separateness. Male. Female.

I parted my mouth and ran my tongue around it, needing air. Gideon nodded as if I'd spoken, turned and took the rifle. I watched him fit the pellet into the breach and snap it shut, then lift the stock to his shoulder. He closed one eye, and the pale-gold lashes swept the freckles on his cheek. He shot. Reloaded. Shot. Reloaded. Shot. Three bull's-eyes. He refused his free go and came back to me. We felt different.

We went on the dodgems and he drove one-handed, holding me tight against him. I cowered and screamed. We went on the Ferris wheel—right up near the low, dark clouds—and he rocked the car till I screamed again. He held me with my face in his neck, and every now and then he would rock the car so that I would push myself against him. Yes, our roles had changed: dominant male, submissive female. I could have stopped it, changed things. But I didn't.

He led me out toward the bulk of the railway station, solid against the dark sky. Here there was a humming from half a dozen turbines generating tinsel life to the fair; huge coils of hose-containing cable tripped us at every step.

We were in last year's reeds, tall and scratchy, brittle but sharp. I could smell a brook or a pond. The din was behind us, offering spurious privacy; the station was ahead, just as impersonal. We were in a no-man's-land.

He started to kiss me. He was shaking and frantic, and at first it made me feel powerful and good. I held his head in my hands and moved it when I needed air, which wasn't often. His hands were everywhere, making me feel slim and alive and desirable and I didn't move them either. Then he started to tug at my jeans.

"Gideon—"

There was no stopping him now. I tried to twist away. He was incredibly strong. I stopped feeling powerful. I felt very weak. And not good. Sort of sick.

"Gideon—not that!"

He froze momentarily.

"Don't you want me? I thought—I thought—"

There was an ache of loneliness in his voice that echoed mine. I kissed him again, desperately.

"Of course I want you. I'm frightened. Don't leave me."

"Oh, Cass . . . oh, Cass . . ."

He drew me against him again and I stumbled because my jeans were around my knees. We landed in the scratchy reeds. I cried out with the pain of them on my bare thighs, and he held me and kissed me and fought out of his jacket and put it under me. Just for a minute I enjoyed it again. And then I stopped enjoying it. Then I hated it. Everything was spoiled and ruined forever. All because of Gideon Jones.

I held back the hysteria somehow.

"Got a tissue?" I asked tightly.

Dimly I saw him shake his head. I went through my pockets and came up with one solitary square. It was inadequate.

He drew a deep breath. "Cass. Was it all right?"

I didn't care anymore that he had given up Sweden to be with me. I never wanted to see him again.

"Absolutely dandy," I said lightly. "My back is bleeding in forty-nine places. You've bruised my ribs, besides . . ." I dabbed ineffectually and spat the final inadequacy. "Besides messing me up completely!"

He sat up straight. Anxious.

"I'm sorry, Cass. Come here, my love—"

I threw away the tissue and pulled pants and jeans hard against my sore crotch.

"Why? So that you can comfort me again? My big brave hero? With his blasted rifle and his . . . other equipment!" I zipped my fly viciously and bent to ram my feet more firmly into my shoes. Then I broke through the reeds and left. My feet went ankle deep into slime; I turned in another direction.

He said, "That day in the coffee shop—don't you remember? You told me I must learn to play your game. I thought that was what it was all about, Cass. Honestly! I thought that was why you dropped out of the trip—Cass, wait! Listen! I'll get my bike and run you home!"

I ignored him, turned yet again, saw the lights of the fair and began to run. This time I spotted the coiled snakes of cables without difficulty and cleared them in frenzied antelope leaps. The Ferris wheel, the dodgems, the rifle range. I burst onto the cinder track that led back to town. My breathing was labored as I loped up the sharp incline of the railway bridge. From its summit a row of lights could be seen negotiating the one-way system out of town. It was a bus. I didn't care where it was going. I took the downhill slope fast and was holding the bus shelter wall, sobbing, when the bus drew in.

"Out o' breff, girl?" queried the driver, holding out his hand for the fare. I couldn't speak. I showed him my bus pass and he nodded briefly. "First stop, C'sbury," he announced. I stumbled to a seat. By great good fortune, it was the right bus. All I had to do was sit still and in forty minutes I would be back in the huge, dark quiet of my hills.

I collapsed and stared through the window. As we drew level with the railway bridge, Gideon Jones topped the rise. I saw the streetlights on his ginger hair. I cowered low and hoped he hadn't seen me.

7

Dad poked at the savory rice.

"Aren't there any chops left in the freezer, Cass?"

"Don't know. It's nearly empty."

"Use it up, chick. We'll go down to Weston one afternoon. Take a picnic and let the kids dig sand castles. Two birds with one stone."

"I don't want to go to Weston."

He was surprised. "I thought you liked it down there. You didn't have a row with Mum?"

"Sort of." That wasn't a lie. I looked down at my plate of rice and remembered I should have mixed in two tablespoons of mango chutney. No wonder it looked insipid. The twins, who had eaten before their nap, had sprinkled sugar on it.

Dad said quietly, "What happened, love?"

"Nothing. It was just awful."

There was a silence. We both chewed manfully. He said, "Are you too old to sit on my lap and have a good cry?"

I sniffed. "Stop trying to get out of eating the rice."

He pretended to look bewildered. "Chick. It's delicious. Honestly." He filled his mouth and pushed the edges of his eyes up into slits. "Lice always dericious."

I was just about to get up and fling myself on his lap and indulge myself in a weep, maybe even a confession, when there was a thunderous knock on the kitchen door. Dad groaned, got up and opened it. Gideon Jones stood there.

He wore a huge and muddy parka, jeans tucked into boots, and his crash helmet was beneath his arm like a skull. The wind flattened him one side, ballooned him the other; his hair stood on end like rusty wire. His pale eyes watered.

He looked past Dad at me and said with truculence, "I've been knocking on the front door for ages. Some kid is screaming its head off upstairs. Are you deaf or something?"

Dad said, "Who the hell are you?"

"My name is Jones." Gideon stared at Dad disapprovingly. "Are you Catherine's father?"

Dad didn't take to Gideon's censorious manner any more than I had. He said, "It looks like it, doesn't it? You'd better come in . . . Jones. Seems as if you've woken up the kids, so there's an end to our dinner hour anyway."

Gideon hesitated, then took a step inside. Dad slammed the door in the teeth of the wind, just missing the parka. He looked round at me. I hadn't moved from the table and I was incapable of speech. It floored Dad. He flapped his hands against his trouser legs.

"Better sit down, I suppose. Friend of Catherine's?"

Gideon glowered at me, obviously wanting to say he was certainly no friend of Catherine's. In the end he shrugged.

Dad looked at me again and got no help. "Well . . . sit down then. . . . Er . . . cold day."

Gideon sat in Dad's chair. Dad stood by the table. Gideon said, "I want a word with you."

It was plain he wasn't talking to Dad. Dad's eyes came round to me again with an expression of amazed incredulity. Faintly from above came Jenny's angry shouts. I said nothing and did not move.

Dad leaned gently toward me. "Cass, dear. Why don't you give your friend some of this delicious rice? He can have mine if he likes. I will pop upstairs and reassure Jenny and Jack that the front door is still intact." He got his head between me and Gideon, and when he saw my eyes properly, his incredulity went away and he said gently, "Come on, Cass. Dericious lice. Remember?"

I smiled slightly and nodded. He waited till I got

up and went to the stove and began stirring, then he walked into the hall leaving the door open. I stirred. In spite of a wooden spoon, the rice was sticking to the bottom of the saucepan. Dad climbed noisily upstairs and Jenny heard him and was blessedly quiet.

Gideon said, "You didn't tell him then?"

I said nothing; I stirred as if my life depended on it.

His voice became bitter. "Is that the way the game is played now? We don't speak?"

I found my voice. "I can't think of anything to say. Not one solitary thing." I lifted the pan and tried to scratch at the bottom. "I suppose you can and you've come here to say it. So get it over with."

From above came rhythmic bumps, then the girls giggling.

Gideon said, "I didn't know you had . . ." I looked at him and his voice died. He jabbed at the ceiling with his thumb.

I swallowed. "Two sisters. Twins. Three years old. And a brother. He's ten."

"Christ. Where's your mother? You baby-sitting or something?"

"Something. Definitely something."

He made an impatient gesture. "Oh Christ, Cass. All this messing about with words. Is that all it is with you?"

I flushed suddenly and hotly. "Better than your way, isn't it? Isn't it, Gideon Jones?" I wanted to drop the saucepan and hold my crotch. I had been sore ever since.

He began to go red too. I watched the freckles merging together and his eyes turn opaque with anger. I watched him search his mind for something to say; something that would hurt me as I had hurt him. He said deliberately, "How was I to know you were frigid?"

I lifted the heavy pan and drew back my arm. He was going to get it. Scalding rice. Straight in his face. There was nothing else I could do.

He realized that. He stood up and threw himself across the table. Dad's unfinished plate snapped under him, the cruets scattered right and left; but as my arm came forward, his was outstretched to meet it. His fingers caught the scorching rim of the pan and wrenched it from me. It fell to the table with an earsplitting crash. He looked down into it; I stared at the top of his head. From above, the silence was electric.

At last he said calmly, "You need something in that rice. It's too stodgy." He rolled off the table and a couple of forks rolled with him.

Dad yelled, "Cass! You all right? What's happening?"

I went slowly into the hall; I was shaking all over.

"Everything is fine, Dad. I dropped the saucepan. No damage. Keep the girls out of the way while I clear up though, okay?"

I went back. Gideon Jones was stirring the rice with

one hand and shaking tomato sauce with the other. I watched while he tasted.

"Okay. Two plates." He glanced round. "Hadn't you better clean up before we eat?"

I stared at the bits of china and rice that had been Dad's dinner. Still like an automaton I cleared it up and fetched two plates. Gideon Jones spooned out rice and we sat down. We ate. When we had finished— yes, incredibly we finished it all—he took the dishes to the sink and turned on the tap. The water jet hit a spoon and flew up and drenched him. He turned it off irritably and wiped the palm of his hand over his face. I pointed to a towel over the stove rail and he took it and mopped.

Then he looked at me over the top of it and said something incomprehensible.

"What?" I asked.

"Will you *marry* me!" he snapped, throwing the towel onto a chair. "That's why I came here today. You'll have to marry me now, won't you?"

I started to laugh. There was nothing else to do. Hysteria bubbled in my nose, ears and throat department, vibrated my diaphragm, made me start to slip off my chair onto the floor. It infuriated Gideon Jones.

"Dammit, you know what I mean!" he snarled. "We didn't take any *precautions* . . . did we?"

My stupid insane laughter dried up. That last little query did it; he was hoping so much—so obviously— that I was on the pill.

I said levelly, "Get out, Gideon. Fast."

"Cass, I'm asking you to—"

"I know what you're asking. No, we didn't take precautions. And no, I won't marry you. I wouldn't marry you if you . . ."

"Were the last man on earth," he finished. His freckles had merged again. He picked up his crash helmet and turned for the door. As he lifted the latch, the wind took the door out of his hand and swung it open.

"I'll be off then," he said into the gale. He felt in his parka and produced a piece of paper and put it on a chair behind the door. "Ring me if you . . . need me. About anything."

He slammed the door behind him.

I picked up the paper, which he had obviously had ready for me. His name, address and telephone number were printed neatly on it. Even as I looked, an enormous salt tear fell on his writing and smudged it hopelessly. So even there we failed to communicate.

I screwed up the paper and burned it as I'd done Alan's check. It gave me just as much satisfaction. Which was nil. I went on crying.

8

Two ghastly days passed. I did try, I really did try. It rained and blew alternately, and when it just blew I took Jenny and Jack for walks and we picked bluebells and wild garlic flowers and late primroses; and when it rained we pressed them between old newspapers and bricks. I made them a den under the kitchen table, and they played house and an endless game called "postie" which entailed mailing and delivering "letters."

Anyway, that awful Easter weekend eventually passed and I wondered what it had been like in Sweden. Or Weston. Last Easter Mum had phoned me and wished me a happy Easter.

The phone must have been telepathic, because just as I reached that thought, it rang.

"Catherine?"

I should have slammed the receiver down immediately. I actually took it away from my ear to do just that; then I put it back.

"Yes?" I said very coldly.

"I wanted to ring before, but Mum and Dad were around and I thought if I went to a box, I'd have to keep shoving in coins . . . so I waited."

"Yes?" I said, still with plenty of dry ice in the voice.

"Well, it was just . . . I wondered if there'd been any . . . sort of . . . misunderstandings the other day." He cleared his throat, drowning my ironic laugh and practically bursting my eardrum; then his voice became very brisk. "It was just that I wanted to make the situation perfectly clear to you. I mean, if you should change your mind or anything. Okay?"

"What are you talking about, Gideon?" I let impatience with a dash of irritation come through the frost.

He said a little less briskly, "I don't . . . I didn't . . . want you to think I asked you to marry me because I thought I *had* to ask you to marry me."

There was a silence. That was what I had thought, of course. I said flatly, without any expression at all, "I still don't get it. Sorry."

He exploded. "Dammitall, it's not that hard to understand, is it? I *want* to marry you! That's all! I *still* want to bloody well marry you even though you said . . . what you said! So, if you ever change your mind . . . well, you've got my bloody phone number, haven't you!"

And *he* slammed down the receiver. He had the actual nerve to hang up on me before I could hang up on him. I stood there holding the phone and staring down at the hobbyhorse until I discovered I was almost grinning. Then I put it down.

The next day Jack said, "Daddy's taking us to Weston on Satty."

Jenny nodded. She had the door open into their den and was just going out for that day's post. "We'll paddle again. Like we did with Cass."

"Daddy won't let us," Jack objected.

"Cass will, though," Jenny reassured her.

I was a soft touch for the twins and a soft touch, in more ways than one, for Gideon Jones. I added liver to the onions I was frying and watched it shrink in agony in the hot fat. Life was grim.

Jenny scurried in with some newspaper cuttings and posted them to Jack. I poured the contents of the pan into a casserole and put it in the slow oven with a rice pudding. There was a mass of dishes to wash. I decided to leave it and make a cup of coffee.

The twins brought their mail to the tabletop to read with their milk. They'd found the old box of snapshots in the front room; the contents were diverting. There were Dad's parents, who had farmed on Mendip all their lives, and died, as Dad put it, in Wellington boots. There were uncles and aunts in uniform; someone on a donkey. The newspaper cuttings were announcements of weddings, funerals, births. I looked through them idly and sipped my coffee.

"Ellerman, Durston," I read in an important voice for the benefit of the girls. "The marriage is announced between Doris Eileen Ellerman and Stanley George Durston. June 26, 1929."

Jenny said, "That's our name. Durston is our name."

I explained. "Stanley George Durston was our grandfather. Daddy's daddy."

Jack passed across another cutout.

"At home. The gift of a son, Jack Austin, to Stanley and Doris Durston of Mayfield Crossing Farm, Mendip, May 12, 1935." I grinned, quite enjoying this. "That's Daddy. Jack Austin." I leaned over. "What else is there? Is my birth there?"

They riffled through possessively and eventually pushed the lot over the table. Yes, there was the announcement of my birth: Catherine Anne in person. Not at home. At Bath Royal United on June 12, 1963. I stared at it thinking that Mum and I had been together then, probably both imagining we should always be together.

I said, "Drink your milk, girls. Then we'd better put this post safely in the box again. Hurry up."

They didn't want to hurry up. Jack indicated another bundle. "We haven't finished yet, Cass." I glanced at them. Deaths. Gran and Grandad Durston. Gran and Grandad Sparling. And another birth, obviously misplaced. I looked at it, frowning. It did not make any kind of sense. It said: "Jack and Kate Durston are proud to announce the birth of a daughter, Deirdre. August 16, 1964. A sister for Catherine."

Deirdre. A sister for Catherine.

I said quickly, "Are there any more cuttings, Jack? Go through the snaps—give them to me—stop it, Jenny, let me do it!" I slapped them away and felt their furious umbrage bombard me as they slipped off their chairs and retired beneath the table. I whipped through the old snaps. Looked again at the cuttings. There was nothing else. Deirdre Durston had not died. Did that mean Catherine still had a sister? Not a half sister, not a stepsister. A whole sister?

Dad finished the liver and sat back replete.

"Crossword?" he said, reaching for the paper.

"Okay." I let him start off. Four letters, two letters. Adjacent. "Next to," he decided, not even glancing at me for confirmation.

I said, "Who is Deirdre, Dad?"

It didn't seem to register. "Of the sorrows?" he asked, still writing. "Have you already looked at this one?"

"No." I decided on further shock tactics. "I'm talking about my sister."

He looked up, met my eyes calmly and looked down again.

"You know already who she is then. Was that why you fell out with Mum last Saturday?"

"No. Mum's kept as mum as you."

He put the paper down but not the pencil. "How then?"

I indicated the box of cuttings. "There's an announcement in there. Of her birth."

"Oh. Yes. Uh-huh." He picked up the paper again. "She died soon after."

I blurted, "There's nothing about that in there. Just her birth. Not her death."

"I don't know whether we had an insertion in the paper. She was . . . a baby." He looked up without any of his usual understanding. "Forget it, Cass. Don't rake it over. It gives—gave—your mother a lot of pain." But his voice was hard. He grinned suddenly. "If it's sisters you want, you've done all right."

I said doggedly, "Mum would have put it in the paper."

"No. No, she wouldn't actually. She wasn't well at the time."

I stared at him wide-eyed. That was when Mum had her nervous breakdown, was it? She had me. Then very quickly another baby who died. Then a nervous breakdown. Then she left. Had it been like that? Had her leaving had nothing to do with me, but something to do with losing her baby?

I blurted my thoughts aloud. "That was why she left . . ."

He flinched back from the table; he actually flinched, his chair rocking, his paper falling into his lap.

I stammered, "Sorry, Dad. I didn't mean—"

"I wasn't right for her. The farm—none of this was right for her, Cass. She met Alan and he was right. Can't you believe that after all this time?"

I'd gone too far. I tried to retrench and recoup. "Can you tell me about Deirdre?"

He picked up the paper. "No. She was dark. That's all I remember."

"Why . . . why did she die?"

He pretended to read a clue while he thought. Then he said, "Pneumonia." He stood up. "I'd better get on." He went to the lobby and I heard him stamping into his boots.

I sat there for ages after he'd gone out. At last I got up and cleared the table. Then I went up for the twins and got them kitted out in their parkas.

"Is the sun shining, Cass?" asked Jenny, staring squint-eyed at the bright window. I raised my eyebrows at Jack and she interpreted for me.

"What she means is are we going out for a walk?"

I picked up Jenny suddenly and kissed her fat cheek.

"Yes, baby. The sun *is* shining," I said.

It was. I didn't believe Dad. Incredible though it might seem, I firmly believed that somewhere I had a sister. A year younger than me. Dark like me. Called Deirdre.

I have wondered since why I was so certain. Was I simply bored—trapped by the twins, cut off from Mum? Was I appalled by what had happened between

Gideon Jones and myself, and did I think this might be a way to resume our relationship on a more practical level? Or did I really intuit that Deirdre was alive and Dad was lying to me?

Whatever the reason, I couldn't do much about it myself, because I certainly was trapped by the twins. And knowing that Mum had had a breakdown about it once before did not encourage me to ring her and ask her point-blank as I'd done with Dad. Dad's reaction had been tense, Mum's would doubtless be more so. So that left Gideon.

I telephoned him while the twins watched Dad do the afternoon milk. Luckily he answered the phone himself.

He said, "I nearly rang you again. In case you'd got rid of that piece of paper the minute my back was turned."

I was amazed—as usual—by his perspicacity. "I did, as a matter of fact."

"Ah. Sometimes I think I know how your mind is working at last." He sounded pleased with himself. "So. How did you get my number?"

"I remembered Redland. There are only fourteen Joneses in Redland. I've rung six of them. Not too bad, really."

"Bad enough." He really did sound cheerful. "So. You've changed your mind? I'll be up and we'll discuss it."

"Changed my mind?"

He said delicately, "About my proposal."

"What? Oh, God . . . Gideon, please forget it. I'm not planning to marry anyone till I'm forty-five. I'm frigid, have you forgotten?"

There was a long pause. He didn't apologize. At last he said brusquely, "So why are you phoning?"

I was going to tell him that it certainly wasn't for the pleasure of listening to his conversation—something on those lines. Then I didn't.

"I want some advice. Objective advice. I'd normally ask Nadine, but as you know, she's away."

I could almost see his puzzled frown; he was looking for the catch.

"I'm not hot on womanly advice, Catherine," he said finally. "What about your mother?"

"My mother lives at Weston and we're not terribly friendly."

"Your mother lives at . . . you mean she's left you with those kids?"

"They're not hers. She's got a son. I told you about him. Anyway, forget my mum—I can't ask her. And Dad's pulled the shutters down on all questions. And as you know, I'm housebound at the moment. So I thought I'd ask you. You told me to get in touch if I needed anything. I need some objective advice."

Another pause. Perhaps he was dimmer than I'd thought.

He said slowly, working it out as he went, "Is that why you couldn't go to Sweden? Because of the kids?"

"Yes. My stepmother is pregnant again and needed a break."

He took ages to assimilate my self-sacrifice, and in the end I had to be honest with him.

"It wasn't quite like that. You wouldn't understand. My mother's husband wanted to pay for me. I couldn't accept that. So when Betty asked me to mind the kids, it seemed like the perfect excuse."

The wires hummed for ages. I said, "Are you still there?"

He said, "You're a complicated sort of a person, aren't you?"

"Isn't everyone? Listen, Gideon, this isn't anything deep or psychological. Or anything. I simply do not know how to go about finding out something."

Another pause. I said impatiently, "Look, this phone call is on Dad's bill! He'd have a fit if he could hear all this waffle!"

"Okay. Go ahead." His voice was now resigned.

I said concisely, "I've just discovered I've got a sister. Dad says she's dead, but I don't believe him. How can I find out?"

There was a funny glugging sound. Maybe he was swallowing.

I said, "Well? If you want an hour or so, perhaps you could ring back?"

He said weakly, "I thought you had two sisters."

"*Half* sisters, lummox! I'm talking about a proper sister. Born just a year after me." I waited. "Gideon, could you pull yourself together? It's not *that* incredible, surely?"

"Actually, you've summed it up, Cass. It is incredible. This is 1981. People aren't hidden away or anything. Are you certain you're not making this up?"

I nearly put the phone down. But I didn't. "I found the newspaper cutting. Besides, Dad has admitted that much."

"It wasn't a miscarriage or something?"

"They don't put miscarriages in papers. And Dad said she died soon after her birth."

"What did she die of?"

"Pneumonia. Dad didn't sound too sure. And not too interested, either."

"It's a long time ago, Cass."

"Sixteen years isn't that long."

"What makes you think he's lying? He seemed a straightforward sort of a bloke to me."

"I didn't think you'd noticed him. You made a good job of ignoring him."

"I was under strain, if you recall."

"Yes . . . yes." For some reason I remembered the water spurting off the spoon into his face and I grinned. "Well, I'm pretty certain he's lying this time. I know him fairly well. He . . . we used to be quite close before he married Betty." I stopped myself. "Anyway, there's no announcement of the baby's death."

"That need not mean much." His voice was almost gentle all of a sudden. Hard to think of Gideon Jones being gentle.

"I think Mum would have . . . she's like that."

"Catherine . . . Cass. Are you crying, for God's sake?"

"No."

"It would be pretty damned silly to cry over some-one you never knew. Who died when you were one year old."

"Who might have died. Anyway, I've only just dis-covered that Deirdre existed, so if she really is dead, I've only just discovered that too. I suppose I'm al-lowed to feel sad as it's only just happening for me?"

He said, "Listen. We'll have to talk about this. If I'm going to do any detective work on your behalf, I need to know more. I'll be up in an hour. How's that?"

It was four-thirty; we'd just got in from our walk. Teatime . . . Dad . . . television.

I said, "Make it two. Dad will put the twins to bed and we can walk up the coombe. It'll be a good sunset tonight."

I wished I hadn't said that. But he didn't seem to notice. He said, "I'll need to know a lot of details. Names and dates, places of birth and so on. You won't mind?"

"I won't have to, will I?" I asked ungraciously.

We walked slowly up the coombe with about two feet of air space between our carefully relaxed arms. He asked me a lot of irrelevant personal questions and I answered him because I had said I would. We didn't quarrel or even get abrasive.

When we got to the top I took him to the place where you can see the lakes on one side and the flat line of the sea on the other. The sunset was marvelous.

It made his ginger hair look fiery red and his eyes startlingly pale against the darkness of his freckles.

He glanced at it all briefly, almost cursorily, and turned away to go back down.

"Right. I've got the maiden name of mother. Date of wedding. Your birth. Baby's birth. I'll start from there."

I trailed after him, disappointed that from my outpourings he had extracted so little.

"What will you do?" I asked curiously.

"I'm not sure yet. Parish records maybe. Registrar. I'll work it out."

"It'll take a lot of your time."

"Plenty of that just at the moment."

I swallowed. "Of course. You should be in Sweden."

"No. That's the one place I shouldn't be."

We walked on in silence. Some rabbits sat up and eyed us from a clump of dock. Gideon said, "Ever read *Watership Down*?"

"Yes." I looked at him and we exchanged a smile.

I said, "Honestly, Gideon, I didn't mean you to miss Sweden."

We came to the gate of the lower paddock and he vaulted it.

"I realize that now. Sorry. Sorry . . . I said those things. All those things."

We didn't speak again until we reached his motorbike behind the barn. He picked up his helmet and turned it in his hands.

I said, "D'you want some coffee? Don't worry about Dad. He's okay."

"No. No, thanks." He put on the helmet and some gauntlets, straddled his bike, kick-started it into frenzied life. Above the roar he said something.

"What?" I yelled.

He throttled down somewhat and bellowed, "You're a very beautiful girl, Catherine!"

Then he left, and the grit from the drive spattered on my jeans.

I didn't hear another thing from Gideon Jones until Friday. All day Thursday he left me without a word: he'd told me I was beautiful, then he left me without a word for a whole day. Then on Friday when I answered the phone for the umpteenth time, telling myself that of course it wasn't him; it might be Betty, it might be the Pollards, it might be the National Farmer's Union, but it certainly wouldn't be Gideon Jones . . . his voice said, "Catherine?"

"Yes?" I hadn't meant to squeak eagerly like that. I modulated my voice, "Yes?" I repeated, basso profundo.

"Listen. Nothing doing at the moment. I'll be away over the weekend. In touch when I get back. Okay?"

He couldn't do this to me. "Are you alone?" I said.

He said, "No."

I said, "Nor me."

He said, "Well . . . that's it, I suppose. Okay?"

I said, "Of course. Okay. Naturally. Cheerio then."

He said, "Cheerio, Cass."

And that was that.

Saturday came and we went to Weston. The sun was almost hot. I wore my bikini and thought I might get a tan. Jenny and Jack went through the whole seaside routine. We dug holes and castles, paddled, bought ice cream. They were marvelous and I loved them, but I was bored out of my head.

I said to Dad, "Isn't it time we went to the freezer center?"

He was trying to read the paper. He said, "The funny thing is, I always wanted kids. I always wanted a big family. But when they start to grow up . . ." He shook his head dolefully and I half grinned, but I wasn't a bit amused. I wanted to say things like: Well, you sure got your wish, two from Mum and two and a half from Betty. Or even: Is that why you got Mum pregnant so fast? And Betty the day after you met her?

I cut off my thoughts quickly and went on grinning.

Dad said, "Listen, chick, the girls are happy here. They're going to hate trailing round the shops. I'm okay too. How about if I sign a check and you go and get what you need? Leave it in one of those insulated sack things and we'll pick it up when it's time to go home."

That sounded a bit better. I grinned more sincerely and put my shirt over my bikini top.

He said suddenly, "You've been a good kid, Cass. Here, take this fiver and buy yourself something." Dad still thinks you can get a model dress for a fiver, but needless to say I took the money gratefully. "Tell you what," he went on. "Treat yourself to a good lunch somewhere. I can give the kids their picnic. Yes, do that, Cass. It's not midday yet. You don't have to get back here till three or four. Have some time to yourself."

Now that *was* a gift. I pulled my jeans over sandy legs and put the check and money in my bag, not hiding my eagerness anymore. When I got up on the prom I looked back at Dad for a long minute. He'd given up the news and put the paper over his head. The twins were pointing and laughing at him and he was laughing back. He hadn't lied about that anyway; he did like kids.

The freezer center was nearly empty. I filled a cart, wrote the check for £65.42 and left the girl to pack the stuff and put it into the cold storage for me. I zipped Dad's bank card into my pocket and set off again, light as air. I wanted to fritter my fiver . . . a record, a Coke, a pastry . . . I was free.

I went into Westonelectric, donned a headset and

listened to five singles, but didn't buy one because I could tape them all off the Top Twenty. The girl gave me a filthy look as I wandered out, and I smiled at her and blew a kiss. Then I went to Oliver's and tried on about ten pairs of shoes. I didn't blow that girl a kiss; I felt sorry for her kneeling down sweating over my stupid feet. I bought a pair of shoelaces just to cheer her up. Then I went in for my Coke, and there, sitting with two other boys, all three of them in Cub uniform, was Mark.

I was delighted to see him. I'd been going through all the people in my mind that I'd like to be with and had forgotten Mark. I was wholeheartedly delighted to see him. And I think he felt the same.

"Hi, Cassie!" He smiled with an adult seriousness. "I was just telling them"—he jerked his head at the other two—"about our raft. They don't believe me."

"What don't they believe?" I hovered over their table wondering whether it would be a liberty to sit down with them.

"That we could make it float with Coke cans. We did, didn't we?"

"We did." I looked at the other two. They said nothing.

Mark chuckled reminiscently. "The bungs must have melted," he explained. "It sank when we left it." He glanced up at me. "Haven't you got any money? I've got enough to get you something."

That was an invitation to sit down, so I sat down. "I'm rich," I boasted. "And I've bought you a present."

82

"A going-away present?" asked Mark.

That brought me up sharp. "Going away?"

"We're going to Ibiza for ten days. It was a cancellation and Dad thought it would be good for Mum to have a holiday. She hasn't been well." He looked round at the staring, curious eyes. "You blokes go on," he commanded. "I want to talk to my sister."

At any other time I'd have wanted to laugh then, but I was too concerned about this news of Mum to do more than just look. The "blokes" got down with much chair scraping and left.

"What's up with Mum?" I asked.

"I don't know. She's tired. She gets tired sometimes and Dad takes her for a holiday."

Oh, Christ. Was it another breakdown? Was it my fault?

Mark said, "What's my present, Cassie? If you didn't know we were going away, why did you buy me a present?"

"I don't know." I fished out the shoelaces. "Be prepared," I quoted the motto of the Scouts.

He loved them. He curled up laughing just like he had that Saturday at Brean. "Nobody bought me shoelaces before!" he crowed.

"Liar!"

"Well, not for a *present*!" He sobered slightly. "I wish you were coming on holiday with us, Cassie. Nobody does special things like you."

I was overwhelmed. "I wish I was too."

He was eager. "Dad could fix it! Dad can fix anything! I'll tell him you want to come and he'll—"

"Don't say anything of the sort, young Mark!"

"Okay." He was sentient, that kid. "Okay, I'll say *I* want you to come!"

I shook my head. "I can't, honestly. College starts next week. Thanks all the same." He looked crestfallen. I said, "I'd rather go on holiday with you than with anyone else. Really. But I can't."

He undid the shoelaces and laid them on the table. "Why doesn't Mum want us to be friends, Cassie?"

I took a deep breath and held it for a moment.

"Doesn't she?" I asked.

He tied one end of the lace to the other and tested the knot carefully.

"She said you wouldn't be coming for a weekend for a while and I mustn't keep asking."

"Well, I was supposed to go to Sweden. Then when I didn't, I was looking after the twins. Jennifer and Jacqueline. You know about them."

"Of course I do. Your father got married again, like Mum."

I watched him tie a knot at the other end of the laces. "Last time we talked you were calling her Mummy."

"I'm older now."

"Yes, I suppose you are." I sighed. "You're ruining those shoelaces."

He said defensively, "They're mine. You gave them to me."

"Sure. Sorry. Go ahead. Knot them up."

He gave a ghost of a grin.

We were silent while he went on fiddling with the laces.

One of the things I had always liked about Mark, long before the flowering of our friendship at Brean, was his quiet acceptance of me. He was never embarrassed in the presence of the big half sister who was such an occasional visitor. His silences had been comfortable. This silence was not comfortable.

After a bit he said, "Walk home with me, Cassie?"

I couldn't do much for him, but I could do that. We stood up and went out into the sunshine together.

He wanted me to go in "for a cup of tea." I was beginning to know what he had in mind, and this time it was some big reconciliation between Mum and me. At last I told him to lay off.

"If Mum's not well, how d'you think she'd feel to see you and me together?" I asked. "If you're really that much older, Mark, grow up! She's mad with me for letting you muck up your uniform that day—you know that as well as I do. So—"

"I told her it was my fault!" he put in hotly. "She said she believed me."

"Okay, she believed you. So she's mad with you for making me muck up my jeans!" I grinned at him. "Listen, Mark, play it cool. Go to Ibiza and have a good holiday and see how the land lies when you get back."

He considered this, stepping delicately on the stones of the pavement in some intricate pattern of his own. His dark-green sweater was brand-new, so the other must have been past repairing. He had wound the shoelaces around his hand and clutched them like a charm.

"Okay," he said at last. "But it's not fair."

"No. Some things aren't fair," I agreed.

We got to where the prom opens into wide grass areas dotted with bushes and dogs. Alan's brass plate winked at us across the green expanse, and we stood, undecided about how to say good-bye.

"You could come round to the kitchen door," Mark suggested, still working things out. "I could make the tea and we could take it down to the shed and—" The Forrest gate opened and someone emerged onto the footpath and stood for a moment relishing the view of the sea and Brean headland. "We could play stowaways. I could get some food perhaps—" It was a woman. An ample, matronly, coiffured woman. She began to walk down the road.

I said, "Hang on a minute, Mark. Who is that?"

He pointed in the direction of my finger, slightly startled by my urgency.

"I dunno. One of Dad's patients. Yes . . . she comes sometimes. I don't know her name. Why?"

A car drew up at the curb. An old-fashioned Morris Minor. She got into the passenger seat and it drove away.

"I thought I knew her for a moment. Couldn't have." I looked down at him and forced a smile. "Tell you what. Nip inside and see if anyone's about. If not I'll come in and have a cup of tea with you."

He was overjoyed.

"Will you, Cassie? Well, Dad will be in the treatment room, of course. And Mum might be lying down. She lies down a lot lately. Or she might be out shopping." He started to gallop across the grass. "Don't go! Stay right here, won't you?"

He sprinted furiously, as if he'd got a train to catch. At the gate he turned and bellowed so that everyone in Weston could hear: "I'll come out and give you a secret signal if it's all clear!"

The only person who missed that was the Lavender Lady. And that was because she was half a mile up the road in a green Morris Minor.

I skulked as unobtrusively as possible. There was a fire hydrant in the thick pungent greenery of a bush; I squatted on it and looked at my watch. It wasn't quite two o'clock. I had a couple more hours before I needed to get back to the beach; it wouldn't take a couple of hours to look at Alan's appointment book on the telephone table in the hall and find out the name and address of his last patient . . . if I could get into the house, of course. Mark was ages. He must have been discovered.

At five past two I followed a woman walking a Labrador and imagined Mark being cross-questioned by Mum and breaking down and admitting I was outside. The dog stopped suddenly over a compelling smell and I nearly fell across him. "Look where you're going, child!" suggested the owner without sympathy. I skirted the dog and began to cross the greensward back to the beach and Dad and the twins.

Mark's voice halloed after me.

He was at the gate, making huge beckoning gestures with his whole arm. The shoelaces dangled from his fingers, unknotted. I ran toward him.

"Mum's out and Dad's just started a half-hour appointment!" he said. "We'll go round the back way, just in case he looks out the window. Mum's left me almond crunchies for my tea! Almond crunchies, Cassie! They're my favorite!"

"Great," I said. "Great."

I followed him into the kitchen and let him put the kettle on before I told him I'd have to go upstairs to the bathroom.

"I'll be back before you've made the tea," I promised.

I was. It took me just two minutes to find out that the Lavender Lady was called Mrs. Rossen-Phillips and that she lived in Westbury. Not far from Nadine.

I went back to the kitchen and drank tea with my half brother and enjoyed myself. Gideon Jones could jump in the nearest lake if he felt like it; I could manage very well without him.

All I needed now was time and freedom. I needed Betty.

"In case we don't see each other till we're grown up," Mark said dolorously on parting, "I think we should make a pact of eternal friendship."

"D'you really want to do that?" I asked seriously, apprehensively.

"Yes." He eyed me cautiously. "Why? Don't you?"

"Oh, yes. But you do realize what it means, do you?"

"I think so. . . . What?"

"You have to give me one of the shoelaces."

"Oh, *Cassie* . . ." He began to laugh, then checked himself and said, "Is there no other way?"

I shook my head very slowly. "None."

He unwound the shoelaces from his hand and gave me one.

"Then so be it," he said.

We laughed, but I thought of his words as I walked back to the beach. Yes . . . so be it. Indeed.

10

Why was I so certain the Lavender Lady would lead me to Deirdre? As I hung around on the green waiting for Mark, it was an intuitive thing; I felt it couldn't be random coincidence that she had crossed my path three times. When I got to bed that night, I admitted that there was only one tiny piece of evidence to back my intuition, and that was all. The Lavender Lady, Mrs. Rossen-Phillips, had mistaken me for someone else that day in the hypermarket. I am dark, and Dad said that Deirdre was dark. Could she have mistaken me for Deirdre? It wasn't very likely, when you consider that I'd been sitting in the shopping cart at the time, chewing a Double Gloucester cheese. But it was all I had to go on. I hardly slept that night, making and discarding plans for finding out a connection between my sister and the Lavender Lady. The big enormous question over every theory I came up with was: Why had it been kept secret all this time? Why had Dad brushed it aside? Why hadn't Mum told me ages ago?

What I should have done was to have waited until Betty got back, gone down to the address at Westbury, introduced myself, put all my cards on the table and asked her what she knew about it. I didn't do that.

The next day dragged interminably. The freezer was full to capacity, so meals were easy; the sun was so warm we could leave the kitchen door open, and the twins ran back and forth, undemanding but always there. In the afternoon Mrs. Tossell, who used to help out in the house Before Betty, called in and asked us to tea the next day. The phone rang and I thought it was Gideon but it was for Dad. I hardly did a thing all day, but when Dad took the twins up to bed at six-thirty, I was exhausted.

The phone rang again. It must be Gideon . . . it must be.

A voice said, "Hello. Is that Cass?"

It wasn't Gideon; it was a woman. Surely all the thoughts I'd been beaming at Mrs. Rossen-Phillips couldn't have called up a response?

"You don't know me, dear. Betty's mother."

Damn. Damn. Damn. "Oh, hello. . . ." What the hell was her name?

"Call me Gran. I'd like that."

"Hello," I repeated stiffly. "Did you want to speak to Dad?"

"Yes, please, dear. It's about Betty. Poor darling has a kidney infection. Most unpleasant. She's terrified of losing the baby, as you can imagine—"

I interrupted this flow very quickly. "I'll fetch Dad."

I did so with a very tight mouth. If this meant that Betty had to extend her holiday, I didn't see how I could bear it.

Dad came back from the phone with a long face.

"Mrs. Creely wants me to go down and have a look at her," he said. "I don't know whether she thinks it's all in Betty's mind or something."

"How much longer is she going to be?" I cried. "My God, am I supposed to give up my whole career—"

Dad snapped to attention. "What career was that?" he asked pleasantly.

"College is fitting me for a career!" My voice was suddenly petulantly defiant. "I don't mind if she's *really* ill, of course—"

"She needed a break, Cass. You could see that."

"Okay. But she's had a break."

His voice was quiet. "Betty pointed out to me that if we had a housekeeper in, we'd have to pay in the region of thirty pounds a week. She wanted me to give you that much. And I said you'd be insulted.

We were one family, and when needed, we pitched in and helped each other. But I can write you a check."

I swallowed. "I didn't mean . . . It's just that . . . well, I want to go back to college on Monday. See Nadine and the others."

Dad relaxed slightly. "Natural enough. I just don't want you thinking you're more wonderful than you are." He gave a tiny grin. "You're slightly wonderful, of course—"

"Shut up, Dad," I said uncomfortably.

His grin widened. "Don't worry. I want her back too. We're planting next week and she always gives me a hand. And in a couple of months there's the hay."

"Dad. She's *pregnant*! And the twins—"

"She helped out when she was pregnant before. And last year she brought the twins along." He gave me a straight look. "A farmer's wife has to help out, Cass. She knows that."

I swallowed again. I hadn't "helped out," and even if I'd wanted to, there wouldn't have been a minute to spare. I thought of Mum, in her knitted dresses and fur coat, with her beautiful Victorian house by the sea. Dad was right; the farm wasn't her place.

Dad went to see the Pollards and arranged for Bill to do the milking and Mrs. Pollard to move in with us. He packed a case the next morning, spoke to his dog in the entryway and left. I watched the Rover bounce up the track and I wondered about him. The man who had played on Weston beach with the twins, who had looked after me and, only the other day, invited me to sit on his lap and cry, was the same man who expected so much from his wives that one of them had had a nervous breakdown and the other was staying with her mother, probably feigning a kidney infection. How could one person be so soft and so hard at the same time?

That afternoon Mrs. Pollard had a nap with the twins and I took the phone into the cupboard under the stairs so that she wouldn't hear me when I talked to Mrs. Rossen-Phillips.

I remembered her voice exactly.

"Bristol double eight two double four," she said musically. "Who is that please?"

"Ah . . . Mrs. Rossen-Phillips?" My own voice was briskly businesslike. "This is Carpenter's of Bristol. The toy shop. You know?"

"Certainly. How is Mr. Carpenter?"

That floored me for a moment. I hadn't dreamed she might know the owner. Somehow I rallied.

"He's on holiday at the moment." I managed a light laugh. "As you know him, he could doubtless have solved our little difficulty for us. Did you enter our Easter rabbit raffle, Mrs. Rossen-Phillips?"

"Raffle? No, I don't think so. . . . I have a number of raffle tickets here. Were you selling them at the hospital?"

"Possibly. The thing is, we have drawn the lucky

ticket with the name Deirdre Rossen-Phillips printed on it. No address. I hesitated to send the prize to your address until I had checked with you."

There was a pause. Then the lavender voice said frowningly, "I do actually know a child called Deirdre. I am wondering whether my housekeeper might have bought a ticket on her behalf . . . but she knows her real name quite well. May I ring you back? My house-keeper is out at the moment."

No, she couldn't ring me back. I searched my bank-rupt mind furiously.

"Have you Deirdre's address, madam? I could tele-phone direct then and save you the trouble."

It didn't make sense, but apparently she didn't no-tice.

"Well, she's one of the children at the hospital, of course. But they won't know whether Miss Jessop bought her a raffle ticket, will they? Don't worry, I'll telephone in about half an hour. And thank you very much for contacting me."

The line went dead. Damn again. Not that it mat-tered; when she rang Carpenter's it would all be put down to a stupid joke. Meanwhile, Deirdre was "one of the children at the hospital." What did it *mean*?

Dad came through at eight o'clock.

I said, "Jenny hoped you'd ring earlier and speak to her."

"I will tomorrow. Six o'clock, okay?"

"Aren't you coming home till Wednesday then?"

I asked incredulously. It was Monday evening. I couldn't get all through Tuesday and half Wednesday like this. My head was throbbing.

"I'm hoping Betty will be well enough to travel on Saturday," he said so brightly that I knew Betty was there. "She says can you cope."

"Of course I can cope. Anyway, Mrs. Pollard is doing everything. The twins think she's marvelous." I coughed in case he thought I was just plain jealous. "Listen, Dad, Saturday is five days away."

"I know. When does Nadine get back?"

"Saturday."

"Oh. Oh, well. Shall I ring Mum?"

"She's gone to Ibiza."

"Has she? Well, that's that then. Anyone else?"

"No." I was going to leave it at that and hope he wouldn't sleep for worry, but then I couldn't. "Don't be daft, Dad. We're all right here. The Pollards are marvelous and the dog is ready to eat any intruders. And I'll leave the intercom switched on."

He said, obviously to Betty, "It's okay. She hasn't got a nerve in her body. Takes after me." He came back to me. "Now listen, chick. You've got my number. Ring any time of the day or night if there's anything wrong. Okay?"

"Okay."

If I hadn't got a nerve in my body, why did my hands keep shaking and why couldn't I sit down with Mrs. Pollard and watch the television? I stood by the back door and looked up at Mendip and tried to

tell myself that nervous breakdowns weren't heredi-
tary.

The next morning Mrs. Pollard went home to see
to her poultry, and I gave the kids some frozen pastry
to roll out while I made a list of all the Bristol hospitals
in the telephone directory.

There was a ring at the front door.

Well, this time it had to be Gideon. I charged down
the hall, leaped over the dratted hobbyhorse and
ripped open the door. It was Nadine.

I goggled at her.

"You're not supposed to be home yet! What happened?"

She drooped against the doorjamb. "Thanks for
the welcome. The bus was packed. Had to stand. I've
had a row with Mum. And now you're overwhelming
me like this. It's too much."

I laughed. My head stopped throbbing. Nadine was
back.

"It's great to see you, kiddo! Come in." I shouted
back to the twins. "Look who's here! Aunty Nadine!
Make another pastry—she's going to stay and have
dinner with us!"

It was bedlam. They made her wash her hands and
put on a bib. She played up to them while I produced
Mrs. Pollard's cottage pie out of the oven.

"Hey, a proper dinner! My God, I didn't know you
had it in you!"

We ate and chattered nonsense and she rolled her

eyes and combed out her piebald hair and asked if we liked her new bra. She hadn't changed.

"The crossing was terrible. But *terrible*, darlings! Aunty Nadine was sick all the way. And when we got there she went on being sick. She couldn't help it, poor brave darling. She was sick on the bus. In the hotel. In the hospital—"

"*Hospital?*" I yelped.

"Yes. She had to go to the hospital and have injections in her . . ." She looked wide-eyed at the twins. "In her sit-upon."

They shrieked. "You mean bottom, Aunty—you are so *funny!*"

"Sit-upon," yelled Jenny. "Sit-upon."

Nadine said with dignity, "That was where Aunty had her injections. Yes. And though she began to get better after them, poor Mrs. Prior was taking no risks. She had her flown home. In a big silver bird—"

"Oh, shut up, Nadine! Are you serious?"

"Never more. The insurance will cover it, I hope. Otherwise it's nervous breakdowns for two. Ma and Pa."

I herded the kids upstairs, and when I got down she hadn't touched the dishes. She'd opened the stove and was sitting in front of it.

"I thought I'd never be warm again. It's heaven to be home."

"Was it awful?"

"Ghastly. Honestly, Cass, I thought I'd had it. Must

have been gastric flu or something, but Prior was rattled too. And as for Morrie . . . he was really worried." She looked smug.

"Morrie? Oh, you mean that Maurice chap. I'd forgotten him."

"Bet you hadn't forgotten Gideon Jones, though?" She snorted at my expression. "Thought not. Well, a piece of real news for you, Cass me ole flower! He didn't come to Sweden. So you didn't miss a thing. Does that cheer you up?"

"I don't need cheering up." I avoided saying that I knew Gideon had opted out of the trip.

"Oh, yes you do. Your face is as long a fiddle. Tell me all."

I drew up a chair slowly and told her almost all. About Mum's nervous breakdown and Betty's extended absence and the Lavender Lady and Deirdre. I didn't tell her about Gideon. There wasn't much point, since I was never going to see him again.

She was satisfyingly agog. But she found all the holes and picked at them remorselessly. Why should Dad lie? Wasn't it possible that Mum's nervous breakdown was caused by the death of her second daughter? Surely that would be a good reason for trying to pretend she had never happened? And just because Mrs. Rossen-Phillips knew someone called Deirdre in a hospital—a child, mind you, not just a girl but a child—why should I jump to the conclusion that she was my sister? And why hadn't I confronted Dad with this fresh "evidence," anyway? And what on earth did I mean by saying that my own father was a stranger?

She went on and on. My head thumped again and my hands shook. She was silent at last, looking at them.

Then she said, "Well, you've got four days, anyway."

"How do you mean, four days?"

"Your father isn't bringing Betty back until Saturday, is he? And today is Tuesday. You tell Mrs. Pollard I'm staying with you, so you won't need her, and you get yourself down to Bristol and make a few inquiries. Go and see this Mrs. Rossen-Phillips and have it out with her."

"What about the twins?"

"Are you deaf or just daft? I told you, I'll be staying, so I can look after them."

"You don't realize what you're taking on."

"You think I'm incapable?"

"No, it's just . . . What about your mum?"

"We really did have a row. I'll phone her and tell her you need me. She likes you. Thinks you're a good influence. That's a laugh, anyway."

I raised a smile. "Would you? Really? Actually, I do need you."

"I can see that. A few days away and everything goes to the dogs." She heaved a huge sigh. "I suppose it's nice to be necessary."

My smile widened into a laugh. I was so *glad* she was back.

11

Mrs. Rossen-Phillips's house was a one-and-a-half-story effort with a view of Blaise Castle behind it and the Shirehampton golf course in front. It was the sort of house that had weekly deliveries of groceries. It should have tickled me that Mrs. R.-P. did her shopping at the barren hypermarket. I was too busy sweating to be tickled.

Needless to say, after Nadine's offer, I hadn't been able to wait. I'd phoned Mrs. Pollard as I scuffed into my shoes. I was going off without a coat when Nadine called me back and told me to put on my hacking jacket in case I needed to "make an impression." Sitting on the bus, I cooked up more schemes for getting into Mrs. Rossen-Phillips's confidence, and failed. She'd be on her guard against any more inquiries about Deirdre; in any case, she'd probably recognize me. I didn't know where to start with the list of hospitals I'd made. So I went to her house at Westbury and waited for inspiration. Nothing happened. I lurked by the gate and counted the burgeoning narcissus in the nearest flower bed. I walked to the next corner and stared down a road of one-and-a-half-story houses, all with their views and flower beds. And I walked back again. I repeated that and felt tears of frustration pushing my eyes out like marbles. I had to do *something*.

On my third patrol someone was weeding in the garden, and it wasn't Mrs. Rossen-Phillips. It must be the housekeeper. And she didn't know me from Adam. I opened the gate and advanced on her.

"Miss Jessop?"

She straightened with some difficulty. She was about two hundred twenty-five pounds, with a face like an old boot. Cracked leather.

"Yes?"

I smiled with all of my body. "I've left the van at the end of the road—"

"I saw you walking up and down." She looked relieved. "All these roads look alike, I know. Are you the girl from Carpenter's?"

My smile wavered. "I—"

"They didn't seem to know anything about it when

Mrs. Phillips rang, and supposed it was one of the local charities."

"Didn't I make that clear? I'm so sorry."

"That's all right. Mrs. Phillips was delighted that someone had bought a ticket for Deirdre and used her name. She's at the hospital now actually."

"Oh. How lucky. I have the prize in the van. Perhaps I can take it along and she can give it to Deirdre?"

Cracked leather can look reassuring and comfortable. I began to tremble again, but this time from relief after the tension of the last hour. Suddenly I'd turned a corner and things were going my way. It was almost too easy.

She said, "You're cold, my dear. Would you like to come in and have a cup of tea? Mrs. Phillips would be only too pleased, you know. She's a wonderful woman."

"Is she? Yes, she must be." Even my voice wobbled. "I think I'd better get on. But thank you."

"That's all right. Thank *you*." She smiled again and more cracks appeared across her forehead and around her eyes. I counted three chins. "What did she win?"

"Win?" I had forgotten my own fairy story.

"Yes. The prize Deirdre won in the raffle. What is it?"

"Oh . . ." What the dickens could I say? "Probably not very suitable. A cuddly toy."

"My dear, what could be nicer? She'll love it. You hurry along now and deliver it and get home to your own fireside. You don't look well."

I almost forgot; then I hung on to the gate and asked desperately, "Which hospital is it, Miss Jessop? I'm afraid I still don't know exactly why Deirdre is . . ."

"You don't?" The concern on the leathery face deepened. "Naturally I thought as you belonged to the charity . . . It's Worrall Hall, my dear. Straight through the village and a turning on the left. It's well signposted; you can't miss it." She shook her head. "You'd better know . . . it's for the terminally ill. You'll never guess it. Everyone is so cheerful and happy. But I'm afraid . . ."

"You mean—" I swallowed convulsively. "You mean it's for people who are dying?"

"Incurable. Yes, dear."

"Then Deirdre is . . . ?"

She sighed. "Yes, dear."

I left quickly. Not only because I couldn't meet her eyes but because I knew now why I had been possessed with a sense of urgency ever since I'd known about Deirdre. There wasn't a moment to lose.

Worrall Hall might have been the manor house of Westbury Village at one time; I don't know. It was Elizabethan, with tall chimneys and a steep roof and beautiful grounds. At one point there was a view through the elms of the Severn Bridge, suspended fairylike over the stretch of water between England and Wales. All the views were like that; exquisitely framed either by foliage or delicate stonework. Someone had taken a great deal of care over Worrall Hall.

I went to the door set in the middle prong of the Elizabethan E and rang the bell. Nothing happened. I stood there helplessly, not knowing what to do. So near and yet so far. It was four o'clock, and the warmth had gone from the April afternoon. I wanted Dad. No . . . no, I didn't want Dad. I wanted Mum. Mum . . . who was suddenly explained to me. And who was in Ibiza.

I pushed at the door and found it open. Inside there was a homely litter of wheelchairs, walking aids, footballs . . . footballs? Beyond them, a glass door gave onto an inner hall, warm dark oak with a staircase on the right and elevator doors beneath it. Teatime chatter came from behind a door on the left; there was a clink of cup on saucer, a burst of laughter; nothing to associate with that frightful description "terminal."

I went on up the stairs, afraid of meeting someone, and came to a sun-filled landing lined with embrasured windows on one side, doors on the other. I hovered again.

A door banged at the far end of the landing and someone came charging along it with an empty tray. She looked like Nadine somehow.

"I'm looking for . . . Mrs. Rossen-Phillips," I stammered as she drew level. Why hadn't I said Deirdre? I didn't know her other name. She might have . . . she *must* have . . . been adopted.

"She was with Deirdre," the girl said breathlessly,

not stopping. "I think she's gone now. You could look into Deirdre's room."

"Which is it?" I called to the head as it disappeared down the stairs.

"Ten," the voice echoed back. And was gone.

Well, I'd got what I wanted hadn't I? I only had to walk along to number ten and go inside and there would be . . .

I got myself along the landing somehow. I was shaking like a leaf and I could hardly breathe. Now that the moment had come, I didn't want it. If Deirdre *was* my sister, then she was going to die and I was going to lose her. I reached the door labeled "10" and stood outside it with my eyes closed. Then I opened it without knocking and stood on the threshold staring in.

It wasn't like a hospital room. The ceiling sloped and the window was a dormer peering out toward the Severn, a mile or two away. There were chintz curtains and wallpaper with roses on it. And in the middle of the room there was a crib.

Inside the crib was a human being. It had dark, spiky, mongoloid hair like Winnie had had at the adult training center in Weston; like I had had when I finger-combed mine in the hypermarket. It had no arms. Hands with not enough digits protruded from its shoulders. It was curled into a ball, so that the hands seemed to be holding the knees. It was turning its head from side to side. The head grinned when it saw me, and a voice croaked: "Dearie!" And when I just stared at it, unspeaking, it repeated as if introducing itself, "Dearie! Dearie! Dearie!"

I heard someone give a gasping indrawn scream. Then I turned and ran.

12

I passed someone on the stairs; the girl who looked like Nadine. She had a full tray this time, and I remember her holding it aside and following me with startled eyes as I crashed by her, taking three or four stairs at a time and leaping the last half a dozen to land on all fours in the dark inner hall. She called something down to me, but I was up and blundering through into the crowded lobby and out into the air. Still no one was about, thank God, but I was terrified of pursuit. I ran across the gravel sweep and took to the grass, where there were bushes and trees. They were no real cover, but I didn't work that out. I ran from bush to bush, bent double, panting and sobbing aloud, frantic with a kind of fear that came from deep inside myself.

To my right and in front of me there came the sound of an engine, slowing to come through the gateway. I swerved away from it, but I must have been spotted because there came a loud shout and the engine was suddenly cut off. I ran parallel to a steep-banked stream now, which must have girdled the grounds like a moat. Behind me the bushes whipped and crashed and the voice shouted again. I left the growth around the stream and struck out for a clump of laurel bordering some kind of enclosure.

"Cass—for God's sake!"

The voice was on my heels. I had some crazy idea that if I could reach the bushes, I would be all right. They would be a sanctuary in the same way as "home" is a sanctuary in the game of tag. I put on a spurt and reached out; a hand grabbed the flap of my hacking jacket; I was falling; the hand was pushing me forward and down. I got hold of a bunch of thick green leaves . . . dark green like the lakes in Mendip . . . I went into them headfirst, and the hand was still there and someone went in with me.

I tried to get my knees under me and scrabble away but couldn't; the fall had taken the wind out of me, and for about ten seconds I lay there hearing my own gasps being echoed next to my right ear. Then I must have twitched beneath that restraining hand, because a voice, husky with effort, spoke.

"Cass. It's me. Stay still, nothing to be frightened of. It's me. Gideon. Just stay still."

I heard myself make a sound like Dad's dog makes when Dad shouts at him, then I started to cry.

I couldn't stop. At first I expect Gideon was embarrassed and lay there, prone, waiting for me to get it over with. Then when I stayed with my face pressed into the fresh mud beneath the bushes, he must have wondered what the hell to do. I felt him kneel and start to lug me upright; I knew there was mud in my open mouth and all round my teeth and up my nostrils. It didn't pull me together or anything like that. I hung like a limp puppet in his grasp and howled again like Dad's dog.

He began to drag me somewhere. I felt something behind my back and leaned into it; it was more foliage. I felt something on my face, around my mouth, at my flaccid hands; Gideon was cleaning me up. I felt a thump on my shoulder, quite gentle, then another thump and a strange, droning noise. Gideon was comforting me.

I cried harder than ever.

His voice said desperately, "Cass . . . stop it. D'you hear me—stop it this minute!"

I didn't stop it, but the old-fashioned, scolding phrase did check me. I went into the hiccoughing, snuffling sob session that at least heralded a conclusion sometime.

He said, "Christ. I knew you'd take it badly. But I didn't think it would be this bad. What did they say to you? Why were you running?"

110

I caught hold of my breath and gasped through snot, tears and spit, "They didn't say anything . . . I didn't speak to . . . I just *ran!*" The next sob couldn't be held any longer; it racked me, then I groaned, "You don't understand—you don't know—"

His hands held my upper arms and pushed my body together again. He said steadily, "I know that Deirdre is alive. You were right. I know that she is handicapped. And I know this hospital is for terminal cases."

That stopped me. I looked up from between those supporting hands and my wild face asked all the questions. He moved me back and forth, a kindly, slow shake.

"Oh, Cass. I'm sorry. I wanted to be the big hero. Make everything all right. And I can't."

I began to cry again, but differently. Big, sad tears poured down my face. Tears for Dad, for Mum, for Gideon. And for me. We all wanted to make everything all right. And we couldn't.

After a bit I said, "Oh, Gideon. She looked like me. I could see it myself. And—that time—when I curled up and tucked my hands under my chin and combed up my hair—"

He said sturdily, "What's wrong with that? You're sisters." He felt me shudder and went on, "So . . . she's ugly. You're still sisters."

"She could *be* me. If it had been me, Dad would have pretended *I* was dead. Just the same."

He didn't have an answer to that one. He held me

111

tighter while I hung my head and sobbed. At the end of it he said, "Come on. I've brought a spare crash helmet. Let's go and get a cup of tea somewhere. You're frozen."

"No. Not yet." I breathed deeply. "I'm all right now. Tell me why you came here. Tell me everything that happened."

His pale clear eyes were narrowed with anxiety; he wore his leathers like he had at Weston, and they were smeared with mud. I tried to smile at him and couldn't, so I put my hand over my shaking mouth and just kept looking at him. He took his hands off my shoulders and sat back on his heels.

"Okay. Okay. But we mustn't stay here too long, Cass. Someone might see us. And Nadine will wonder what is happening."

"Oh, God. Nadine."

"She didn't know you'd be here of course. She gave me that woman's address and I inquired. They seemed to know you—"

I began to laugh and he thought I was hysterical and grabbed me again.

"It's okay, Gideon. Honestly. Just that . . . poor Mrs. Rossen-Phillips must be wondering what the hell . . . She's a good woman, Gideon. A good woman." Just saying that brought more tears, so we had another pause.

Gideon resumed at last.

"I did the obvious. Parish records at Mendip Church. There it was: marriage of your parents, your christening, Deirdre's christening. No record of a funeral." He waited. "Is this awful? Shall I shut up?"

"No! No, I want to know. I thought you'd forgotten all about it—written me off as a nutter."

"Idiot."

I did an upside-down smile and nodded.

"Well, anyway. That meant she'd come home for a while. To the farm. People ought to remember her." He sighed, doubtless recalling the embarrassing chore of detecting. "The vicar had changed, of course. But his housekeeper had a vague recollection of Deirdre Durston. She'd been taken ill, rushed into the hospital and died there. So the funeral must have been in Bristol." He shifted and his boot gouged a channel in the mud. We were in a mess.

"I went to the Registrar's office in Cheddar and met with a very unhelpful bloke. He told me to go to London. Somerset House. There was a cheap day return on Saturday, so I went then."

Saturday. When I'd gone to Weston and thought Gideon was enjoying himself somewhere for the weekend.

I whispered, "Oh, Gideon. I'll pay you back."

"Don't be *stupid*. Please. I found out that Deirdre was alive. Definitely." He smiled. "I hadn't believed you, not really. You and your feelings . . . but you were right about that." He sighed again. "So I came home and wondered what to do next."

"I wish you'd phoned again."

"So do I now. But I wanted to—to *solve* it. To hand

the answer to you on a plate. Show you how clever I was." He snorted a derisory laugh. "Gideon the Great. Sorry, Cass. I could have saved you this."

"No. No, you couldn't actually." I stood up, aching, and stretched. "Go on talking. Tell me everything. What did you do on Sunday?"

"Went out with my family. They were worried. They were getting suspicious. I didn't want to tell them anything—it's your business, after all. But . . . well, they're okay."

I glanced sideways at him. He had a whole life without me. And he had to get mixed up in this.

"While I was with them I thought about it. Every angle. Even whether Deirdre might have been murdered!" He laughed again at himself. "Monday morning I thought she must have been adopted. Then someone told me if she'd been adopted it would have been on her birth certificate. So I was back to square one again."

I stumbled and he put an arm around me very tentatively. I leaned on it. We walked back across the grass.

"Then I went to our doctor. Nothing to do with Deirdre. I had to see him for a repeat prescription of Ventolin—I'm asthmatic—"

"You're what?"

"I get asthma. Not often."

"I didn't know," I marveled.

"Well, anyway, our doc's been pretty good trying different treatments. I can talk to him. I didn't tell him any names but I gave him enough information for him to make some suggestions. He said three things: death, adoption, handicap." He guided me away from the stream to where his motorbike was jacked up on its stand.

"That had to be it, Cass. It was the reason your father pretended. It was the *only* reason that fitted everything. The doc said it took some people like that. They try to forget it."

He handed me a helmet, then took it back and put it on for me. He sagged at the knees, buckling it carefully, frowning.

He said, "I spent last night on the phone. Then again this morning. Worrall Hall isn't listed as a hospital for the handicapped. So it was last on the list."

He straightened and looked at me. "Maybe this—" He jerked his head. "Worrall Hall . . . maybe it's for the best, Cass."

I held back the tears. "Gideon. Am I going mad? Do *you* think I'm going mad? My mother did, you know."

He grabbed me and held me against his chest.

"I don't thing you're going mad, Cass. But if your mother did, then can't you begin to see why your father tried to push it all away? Wasn't it because he loved you and didn't want it to happen to you?"

I shook my head, not knowing. He got me on the pillion seat and wrapped my arms around his waist. Then he kicked the bike into life and we roared down that beautiful gravel drive and away from Worrall

Hall. I thought of the views framed in stone and foliage and wondered whether we were flashing in and out of sight of the dormer window in number ten. I sent thought waves to Deirdre. My sister.

13

It was marvelous to wake up and hear Nadine coping with Jennifer and Jacqueline. I was so tired I wanted to die. Someone had switched on the intercom and Jenny was saying—already mimicking Nadine's voice to perfection—"What some blasted wevver, Naddie." I smiled into my pillow and lifted my head to study the clock. It couldn't be ten to ten. Jack said, "Kin we have our breakfast now, Naddie?" And in reply to both of them Nadine said bitterly, "Let it rain all day if it wants to. It'll take me that long to find out about this blasted furnace thing!" There was a horrible clang—the stove plate being dropped—then she said furiously, "Haven't you got an electric kettle or *anything*? Just to make one solitary blasted cup of tea?"

I hung out of bed and flicked the switch. "Hold everything. I'm just coming."

I switched off before she could tell me I'd just stopped her heart beating, and put on yesterday's clothes. The mud had dried on the seat of the jeans and might brush off. It was ten o'clock when I joined them in the kitchen.

"I got up at the crack of dawn," Nadine said, both defiant and accusing. "And I haven't stopped, so don't look like that."

"I wasn't." I grinned wanly as the kettle began to sing. "Don't worry, I felt like you do for the first few days. And I had Dad to help me. I don't know how Betty copes."

We drank five cups of tea between us while the twins ate cereal and toast. Then I set up their den and Nadine and I started peeling potatoes. She didn't ask any more futile questions and we didn't mention Gideon. Just before lunch Dad rang because he said I'd sounded funny last night.

"Funny funny?" I asked to stave him off.

"Very." He waited, then said, "We'll be home three days from now, chick. Okay?"

"What time?"

"About two. We'll have a pub lunch somewhere."

"I'd like to go out. If that's all right. About three."

"Sure. You've done your stint. Nadine home?"

"She came early. She's here with me."

118

"Ah. That's why you sounded funny. She has that effect on you."

I said, "Cheerio then, Dad."

Gideon came for me at two. We drove to the village and bought an acrylic rabbit. I had my nail scissors with me, and I cut off the ears when we got outside the shop and stuffed them in my pocket with Mark's shoelace. Then we went on to Worrall Hall and found a parking lot in the old stable yard next to a pump. There was no sign of a green Morris Minor. It was another decent day, and several wheelchairs were being pushed over the grass; two seven-year-old boys were playing football. Miss Jessop had been right yesterday: You'd never know that the people here were here to die.

We saw two male nurses on the way upstairs; they both grinned and said good afternoon. Someone on the landing in a very starchy uniform asked if she could help us.

Gideon said, "We've come to see Deirdre Durston."

The Sister or Duchess or whatever said, "Ah, yes. You've brought the prize, I see. We did wonder. Now, dear, may I be officious and make certain it's suitable?"

I took off the cellophane. "I cut off the ears," I said hoarsely.

"So you have. Now that *was* thoughtful." She turned the rabbit between her hands admiringly. "Nothing dangerous here at all. If only everyone would realize . . ." She beamed at me. "It's been such a mix-up with this prize, hasn't it? Mrs. Phillips was speaking about it only yesterday. Do you want to give it to Deirdre yourself?"

Gideon glanced at me and said, "Yes, please."

"Then follow me."

Obviously the girl who looked like Nadine hadn't said anything, because the Sister/Duchess thought we didn't know the way. She glided like a ship in full sail to number ten and opened the door very gently.

"Ah. She's asleep." She went over to the crib and touched the wiry hair. Not to wake her. I don't think she knew she'd done it. "Would you like to sit for a moment?" She smiled at Gideon. For the first time I realized he was wearing decent trousers and a hand-knitted sweater under his parka. He was looking respectable for my sake. "I'll ask someone to bring you some tea."

She brought up chairs, and we sat down and peered through the crib bars. I held the rabbit on my lap. She sailed out again, smiling at us brightly over her shoulder, closing the door bit by bit.

Gideon said, "She's not ugly, Cass. She's not a bit ugly."

"It . . . it's better . . . when she's . . . asleep."

He looked up. "You're not crying again? Oh, Cass."

"It's not Deirdre. It was *her*. She seemed to love her."

"Oh, Cass. You're so blind sometimes. Of course she loves her. And that Mrs. Phillips—she loves her too."

I kept swallowing like a crazy thing.

"It was just . . . she seemed so alone. Dad had forgotten her almost. And Mum. And I never knew her, and when I saw her yesterday, I felt sick. And I ran away."

He took the rabbit from me gently. "Well, you're not running away now. You're here. Stand up and look at her."

I did.

It was like looking into a slightly distorted mirror. The eyes pulled up into the hairline, the nose was flattened, the tongue protruded from the pouting mouth. I swallowed again, then put my hand into the crib. I touched the blanket with my fingertips. Then I leaned lower and spread my hand so that I could feel the hunched knees through the coverings. I flicked a glance at Gideon and found him watching me intently.

"Don't stare," I whispered. "I can't bear it."

"Sorry." He looked away and down at Deirdre. "She's dreaming."

Her face was twitching, and behind her lids her eyes rolled. I removed my hand quickly and waited, holding my breath. She opened her eyes. I straightened and withdrew. We stared.

"Dearie!" It was the same awful squawk. "Dearie! Dearie! Dearie! Dearie! Dearie! Dearie! Dea—"

Gideon said loudly, "Take her hand! Do something, Cass. Tell her—"

The squawk did not stop. "Dearie! Dearie!"

I could not bring myself to touch one of those

ghastly appendages that were attached to her shoulders like flippers. In the face of that incessant call, like a mynah bird's imitation, human yet not human, I flinched.

The door opened and the Sister came in fast. She went to the other side of the crib and leaned over, cupping Deirdre's face in her red hands.

"It's all right, Dearie. We're here. It's all right." She looked up. "Don't worry. Slip away now; she'll be all right."

Gideon stood up; I was already halfway to the door. He said, "Sorry." He leaned over the crib. "Sorry, Deirdre. This is for you. From Cass. From Catherine, your sister." He put the rabbit down, then picked it up again and touched her face with the soft fabric. She was still, blessedly still, then a coo of unmistakable delight came from the crib.

Gideon joined me and we left.

He and Nadine were marvelous. They made tea and kept the twins occupied until it was bedtime. Nadine put them to bed and he talked to me.

"Don't keep crying, Cass, please. You're asking too much of yourself, that's all. If only you'd tell them who you are, they might help you to adjust."

"You did that! You had the guts to be honest and straightforward. I can't *be* like that."

"Give yourself time. Tomorrow we'll go down again and we'll sit quietly with her for a few minutes."

"I can't touch her. I can't, Gideon."

"All right. The next day you'll be able to."

I pulled myself together and went to talk to Dad on the phone. And then Gideon left, and Nadine and I sat by the stove. I was as cold as she was.

The next day they had wised up on us and we weren't allowed in to see Deirdre. Gideon did his best.

"Catherine is Deirdre's sister, do you know that?" he asked the woman in the green coat who seemed to be guarding the stairs.

"Yes, it would seem possible." She smiled at me nicely. "There is a similarity. However, Deirdre isn't well. We are contacting her mother, and perhaps you will be able to visit with her."

"My mother is on holiday," I said. "In Ibiza."

"Perhaps Mr. Durston—"

I turned and went out and waited for Gideon by the motorbike.

"They're lying," I said.

"Why should they lie?"

"Everybody does."

"Balls."

"Yes, they do. Not you. Maybe not Nadine. But—"

He picked up his helmet and stared into it. "You told me that your stepfather wanted to pay for you to go to Sweden but you wouldn't take it."

I kicked at the gravel. "He's like that. It makes him feel good. I wasn't going to give him the satisfaction of—"

He put his foot on mine. He was wearing his boots and I stopped kicking.

"Stop it, Cass. Just stop it. Can't you see where you're going?"

"I don't know what you mean. Get off my foot."

He got off my foot. "You know what I mean. You're making yourself . . . ugly."

I looked up, startled. His pale eyes were censorious again.

"You won't let yourself believe you stayed behind to look after the twins, will you? You won't be . . . kind to yourself. Nor to anyone else. Maybe your step-father *wanted* to treat you to Sweden because he likes you."

"Well, I don't like him."

"Why not?"

"It's obvious isn't it? He took Mum away."

"Oh, come on. It takes two to tango. Your mum was ill, wasn't she? Maybe he saved her life. Have you thought of it like that?"

I was silent, remembering Mark saying, "Dad could fix it! Dad can fix anything!" Mark loved Alan.

Gideon sighed abruptly and rammed on his helmet.

"People are . . . just people, Cass. They do the best they can. If you expect them to do more, you're never going to be able to forgive them."

It wasn't much good saying anything else. He kicked the bike and we went home. As we went to the back door, I turned to him bitterly.

"Is that what it's all about? Forgiving everyone all the time?"

He wouldn't soften. His eyes looked like clear cold water over gray stones. He said crisply, "Just like they forgive you, Cass."

Friday he arrived at nine-thirty and we made banana sandwiches and went up to the winter picnic place. He and Nadine took off their boots and rolled up their jeans and waded into the harbor we'd made. The twins lugged flat stones from an old dry stone wall and helped make a causeway. I sat by the picnic basket and knew how Mum had felt; split in half. Loving this beautiful old farm, yet hating it. Wanting to see Deirdre, yet frightened at the very idea. Longing to be with people again and knowing she was out of step with them. I could feel myself fragmenting inside. Was this schizophrenia? Nadine yelled at me to pull my finger out and give a hand, Gideon said something about mixed metaphors and Jack ran off to pick me a bunch of celandines. I did all the right things: grinned, shouted something back, accepted the flowers. But I wasn't there.

After the picnic we went back to the farm and made tea for Bill Pollard, who had arrived to do the milk. It was like a party. The phone rang and I thought it was Dad, so I trailed into the hall, glad of an excuse to escape.

It was Mrs. Miller.

"Cass? Dear . . . is Nadine all right?"

"Yes. Fine. D'you want to speak to her, Mrs. Miller?"

"If she . . . Do you think she wants to speak to me, Cass?" I suddenly realized that Mrs. Miller, bleached and rouged Mrs. Miller of the Dying Duck, was near tears. "We had the most awful row, dear. I said some terrible things. I don't know how I've got through the last couple of days without her."

"I'll fetch Nadine."

She came to the phone with a set mouth, but her eyes were wide. She listened hard while I went down the hall and opened the kitchen door, then she gave a sort of sob and said, "Mum, of *course* I do—my God, you're my *mother*!"

I closed the kitchen door softly behind me. Forgiving. I thought of the word as I started to wash the dishes. I split it up. For. Giving. It still made sense.

Gideon took Nadine back home that evening and Mrs. Pollard returned. She put the twins to bed and tut-tutted over the state of the bedrooms. The next morning she spring-cleaned the house before Dad and Betty turned up.

Dad hugged me while Betty cuddled the twins. Then he hugged the twins and Betty kissed me on the cheek. She looked worse than when she'd gone; white and shivery. I opened the stove doors again and pushed a chair close. She sat on it gratefully. She wouldn't have done that before. After our midday dinner, Gideon arrived.

Dad shook hands and introduced him formally to Betty and the twins. The twins laughed uproariously. "We knows Gideon," Jenny informed Dad. "He's been here all the time."

Dad flicked me a funny look and said, "I see."

"Gideon has come to take me down to Nadine's, Dad. Is that all right? I did ask you on the phone."

He remembered me asking. "Nadine's?" he probed, looking at me for reassurance.

"You can ring Mrs. Miller if you like."

He looked surprised, then smiled. "I don't need to do that, Cass. Have a good time."

They met us at the foot of the stairs. The green lady and a man in a white coat. He spoke.

"Miss Durston, is it? We thought you might have felt excluded on Thursday, so we've been looking out for you."

Gideon said, "We can see Deirdre today?"

White coat shook his head regretfully. "She has to be kept under sedation. There are breathing difficulties. But if you would like to chat about Deirdre herself, Mrs. Rossen-Phillips suggested that she—"

"You told her?" I put in swiftly. "You told her I was Deirdre's sister?"

"Well, yes. She was rather bothered about this raffle business and was relieved when it was cleared up. She'll be along in a minute and you could have a cup of tea in the office. She knows Deirdre better than we do, because she always visited her in the other hospital. Before Deirdre came here."

Gideon was smiling as if the afternoon tea were already arriving.

I gasped, "No. No—I can't see her. I'll phone. Thank you. Good-bye." I turned and went through the lobby as quickly as I'd done the first time.

Gideon found me in the parking lot.

"What the hell was all that about? I thought you'd like to hear about—"

"Don't you *see*? She knows about me! All that stuff about Carpenter's—she *knows*!"

He said helplessly, "But she understands! You goon—you heard what the doctor chap said! She's relieved there's an explanation."

"I can't face her. Hurry up, let's get down to the Dying Duck."

But we were too late. Before we'd got our helmets on, the bull nose of a Morris Minor, driven by Miss Jessop, edged carefully into the stable yard. She tapped her horn in recognition and stopped right there, blocking the entrance, while Mrs. Rossen-Phillips got out and advanced on us.

"My dear child!" She was beaming as if we were old, old friends. "I'm so glad . . . so very glad." I thought she was going to gather me to her lavender bosom, but she just took my numb hands and sort of pumped them up and down. "Oh, it makes everything all right somehow!" Her blue eyes were shining. "It makes everything wonderful! That Deirdre has a sister! How happy she must have been to know that. What did she say?"

I looked at her like an idiot. Gideon said, "Mrs. . . . er . . . Catherine is upset, I'm afraid. Um . . . actually Deirdre didn't . . . she sort of called out her name."

Mrs. R.-P. was transported. "Then she knew. Oh, she knew—she knows so much, you see. That's her way of . . ." She squeezed my hands quite painfully. "Catherine. Why don't you come back home with Miss Jessop and me? Your young man could follow on his motorbike. We could have tea in comfort."

I didn't say a word. Gideon said, "But you were going to visit the hospital."

"I go most days. There are others to help." She drew me to her and put her hand in my arm. "Please come and have tea with us. It would give us great pleasure."

Gideon said, "Then, of course . . . Are you all right, Cass?"

I looked up at him and nodded. Miss Jessop folded her seat forward, and they tucked me into the back of the car as if I were an invalid. And we drove back through the beautiful park and down to Westbury.

The one-and-a-half-story house was full of beaten brass trays and Persian rugs on polished parquet. There was a gas fire that looked like burning logs and a teapot that looked like a thatched cottage. The tea was hot and sweet and I began to feel less icy.

Mrs. R.-P. was a large woman and shouldn't really have had tea and scones in the middle of the afternoon. Her cashmere sweater only partially concealed little rolls of fat above and beneath her bra, and her tweed skirt made her bottom look the size of a barrage balloon. But she really did smell of lavender, her nearly white hair was silky and pretty and her eyes were strangely innocent.

"Isn't this nice?" She refilled the cottage pot from a beehive hot-water jug. "I've so often wished that Deirdre could come and have tea with me. And now . . . well, you understand, Catherine. You're going to live for her, really, aren't you, dear?"

I didn't know what she was talking about. Gideon reached across and took my hand, but I didn't need comforting.

She refilled my cup and heaped in the sugar.

"I was pleased when your poor mother went away for a bit of a holiday. I could see the strain was telling. On the other hand, it was a shame for Deirdre. I went each day of course, but it wasn't the same. And then you turned up. It seemed . . . meant."

Gideon said, "Cass hasn't known about her sister. They didn't tell her."

"Well, it takes people different ways, dear." She smiled at him. "Some people won't acknowledge that they have had a handicapped child, you know. Others make themselves slaves to it and ruin the rest of their family life. Who knows what to do for the best?"

"Quite," said Gideon, glancing at me.

I spoke at last. "Is Deirdre going to die very soon?"

"I cannot say, Catherine." Mrs. R.-P. did not meet my eye. Miss Jessop came in with a sponge cake on a silver dish. She put the cake down, came behind me and gripped my shoulder.

"She has a right to know, Rowena," she said sternly. Then, to me, "Tonight. Maybe tomorrow. She is heavily sedated and will simply sleep on, my dear."

Gideon's grip hurt and Mrs. R.-P. looked at me wide-eyed. I didn't feel a thing. I sipped my tea. Then I looked up at Miss Jessop and said, "Thank you."

We sat in Nadine's bedroom and listened to the call "last orders." Gideon said, "You can't do it, Cass. The place will be locked up. There's no point—"

Nadine said, "Please don't do it, Cass. She's seen you, and according to the Lavender Lady, she knew who you were. That's enough."

"I wish I hadn't told either of you. I'm going. That's all there is to it."

Gideon hit his knee. "Why? For God's sake, why?"

"I don't know—don't keep *saying* that! Christ, Gideon. She's got a mother and a father and a sister. And she's on her own there. Christ. Can't you *see*?"

Neither of them said anything to that. Beneath Nadine's window someone called out, "Wait for me!" I sat up suddenly. But of course it was only a customer.

Gideon stood. "Okay. I'll take you."

I shook my head. "There'll be trouble. I don't want you involved."

"I said I'll *take* you. I'll go and wait down the road. How long will you be?"

It was Saturday, so closing time was eleven o'clock.

131

I looked at him for a long three seconds, then gave in. "I'll be twenty minutes," I said.

He left. Nadine said, "Cass . . . this is awful."

I looked at her. Her piebald hair and bright brown eyes. I said, "I'm glad you're okay with your mum now, Nadine. And . . . thanks."

14

Gideon was waiting. It was very dark and he was under a streetlight, looking sinister in his leathers. He handed me a helmet without speaking, kicked the bike and waited for me to climb onto the pillion. I put my arms around his waist and rested my head between his shoulder blades. I wasn't tired, but I hadn't slept well for two nights and things were strange. I was living somewhere in my head . . . or someone was. I mean my head and body kept operating when they should have collapsed. I wanted them to collapse. I tried to imagine waking up in a hospital bed with everyone fussing around me and meals on trays.

We left the bike just inside the gate and walked on the grass by the edge of the gravel drive. Gideon went in front. We didn't speak. Strangely, though it was so dark on the way and down the drive, when we reached the open sweep girdling the house, we found it bathed in milky-blue moonlight. It highlighted the ancient Elizabethan stone and glinted on the mullioned windows. It was quiet. Blissfully peaceful. The words "terminal hospital" attained a grand dignity in connection with this place. Everyone is terminal, after all.

We hesitated in the shadow of some laurels and looked at the door. It was most definitely closed. It had studs all over it.

Gideon touched my arm and began to walk around the sweep toward the stable yard. He trod lightly across the gravel and waited by the old pump, then he turned and beckoned me.

"Staff door," he muttered close to my ear.

There were half a dozen cars in the yard; he disappeared among them, was gone for a very long minute and returned.

"It's locked. We'll have to wait until someone comes out for something. There's no other way in."

We waited. The moonlight didn't penetrate the enclosed yard, and the blackness made it feel cold. Gideon shivered beside me, and I could hear his breath rasping in his throat. I remembered he had asthma sometimes.

Then quite suddenly a light sprang up above the

roof of one of the cars. A small latticed window was illumined for us like a stage set. We could see a section of a kitchen. A row of stainless steel saucepans on a shelf, a massive colander suspended beneath. Gideon left me and slid around a bumper for a closer view. The light went out.

He returned. "Catherine, it's hopeless—we'll never get in. It's a skeleton staff and they won't be coming out until the day shift arrives."

I said, "I'll knock. Make a fuss—insist—I've got to do it."

His sigh was grating. "All right. Listen. *I'll* knock. Tell them I'm lost—ask if I can phone—try to get in. If I do, I'll make sure the door is unlocked for you. I don't like it. I wanted to stay with you, but there's no other way."

"Go on then, Gideon. Please. I'll be all right."

I did not doubt that he would do it, but even in my curiously suspended state, I knew that the method he used—a surefire one—cost him a lot. He used his weakness. He used his asthma.

When the door eventually opened to his knocking and two male nurses stood there belligerently, he was doubled up and his breathing was awful.

"Sorry, mate—" he gasped. "I'm lost. I'll be all right in a minute." He lifted his face to them and in the light from the open door I saw it clearly. It was livid.

They took an arm each and hustled him inside. A minute later I saw them at the kitchen window lowering him into a chair. They hadn't even closed the door.

I slid inside and found myself in a stone-floored corridor. The kitchen was on the right. I went straight past it and down toward a staircase at the bottom. I was halfway up it when one of the nurses went back, closed and bolted the door and returned to the kitchen. I heard him say something about a cup of tea, then that door was closed too. I was on my own.

I found the long landing without difficulty. It was lit by low-wattage bulbs at either end, but there was no need for artificial light because here the blue moon came through the line of windows and washed the oak paneling, the ceiling, the polished floorboards and the line of doors with its dead radiance. Number ten was picked out luminously on Deirdre's door. I stood by it for ages, my ear against the paneling, and was just about to turn the handle when a chair scraped inside. I bolted back to the top of the stairs and crouched. The door opened and a nurse appeared. She stood staring through one of the landing windows at the moonlit park, then turned and walked the other way and went in another door, presumably number eleven.

I whipped back, eased the door handle round in my palm and pushed the door gently. The room looked exactly as I had last seen it, except that the chintz curtains were across the dormer. I slid inside. At the very top of the door there was a small bolt. I picked up the nurse's chair, placed it in position, stood on it and slid the bolt. Then I went to the crib.

The covers were neatly under Deirdre's chin, and her malformed hands looked normal, like a child's upflung in sleep. Tucked against her cheek was the earless rabbit. I leaned on the crib rail and stared down at her. The more I stared, the less odd she looked. I could see our likeness and it no longer filled me with horror. Maybe I was still in my nonfeeling state; I don't know. After a long period of staring I put a tentative hand down, as the Sister had done, and touched her hair. I probably imagined the tiny smile. Her tongue was still protruding anyway, and that made her face lift slightly. I stroked the hair. It was coarse. My hair is coarse. So is Mum's. I pushed it very gently against her scalp with the palm of my hand and released it. It sprang up again. Mine does that.

I stood there with my hand touching her hair until I felt my legs begin to shake. Then I fetched the chair and put it by the crib again, and releasing the catch a millimeter at a time, I let down the side. I sat down.

Another block of time passed. During it I somehow managed to put my finger on Deirdre's tiny palm. It was very smooth, rather cold but certainly not reptilian as I had half expected. I slid my thumb underneath the three knuckles and held it lightly. I was holding my sister's hand.

I went on holding it. I became tired and my head pulled my body forward. I released Deirdre's near hand and took the far one. Then I rested my left shoulder uncomfortably on the edge of the crib and put my head by hers on the pillow. As she was lying in her curled, fetal position, this brought our eyes within six inches of each other. I kept mine open and watched her.

Time went on and on. I couldn't envisage the night ending. The light was on and the curtains were drawn, so there was no way of telling whether the moon had gone. My watch was somewhere beneath my left shoulder. I did not want to know the time anyway; it had long ceased to matter, together with many other things. But I knew what the clatter on the landing probably meant. Patients were washed and changed at unearthly hours to conform with hospital routine; it could be any time between four and six. I did not move. I kept my eyes on Deirdre's closed lids and lay very still, my right arm across her body, my big thumb and four fingers holding her three. The clashing came closer.

In spite of myself, the breath caught in my throat when they tried the door and found it bolted. It was a slim, modern brass bolt, not the heavy kind, and it jarred fragilely as the oak door tried to snap it. There was a pause. Then another try, and another. Then a startled voice outside said, "Sister, can you come? The door seems to be stuck in some way." A second later the handle was turned with irritable authority and the bolt clicked and held. Push. *Click.* Push. *Click.*

How long before it gave?

There was a nonplussed pause outside. Sister's voice said, "Is anyone there?" A rattle. "Answer me, please. Who is in there?"

Involuntarily I pressed Deirdre's hand as if asking for her silence. And I thought her hand pressed back. She lay still, eyes closed, the peculiar half grin like a quarter moon pushed up by her tongue. It was exactly as if she knew. As if we were conspirators. All our childhood celebrated in that macabre game of hide-and-seek.

There was another, much longer pause, then steps and other voices saying things I couldn't hear. I began to count. In a whisper, sharing the tension with Deirdre, I began to count the seconds. How long could the door hold out . . . how long could we hold out?

I had reached seven hundred and eighty five when a familiar voice called to me. I felt my eyes stretch in panic.

"Cass. It's me. Gideon. I've told them everything. And they will wait until your father arrives, if you will just tell them that Deirdre is all right."

I didn't speak. I lay there, staring at Deirdre, quite certain that her fingers were curled around mine.

Gideon said, "Cass, I know how you feel. But if you don't answer, we'll have to knock the door down. And that won't be good for Deirdre, will it? Is she all right? Her pulse? Her breathing?"

I lifted my head, panic at me again. A pulse in her neck fluttered as I pulled down the covers; it subsided and fluttered again. I detached my fingers and tried to stand up, and couldn't. My left arm hung uselessly by my side and there was pain in my chest and my hip and my feet. I forced my head round.

Gideon began again. "Cass, we can't wait much longer. You could be ill yourself. If you're conscious you must speak to us."

I called out, "She's okay. Don't knock the door down. Please. She's okay."

There was a sort of moan of relief from the other side. Gideon said, "Thank God, Cass. Your father should be here in a few minutes. You'll open the door for him, won't you?"

I couldn't bear the thought of Dad. I said, "He can't get here till midday. There's the milking and—"

"Nadine phoned him, Cass. When we weren't back, she phoned him and told him. He'll be here by four-thirty at the latest."

I looked at the door, then back at Deirdre. Gently I disengaged my fingers from hers and began to massage my left side. After a very few minutes I could stand up. I carried the chair to the door, stood on it and slid the bolt back. Then I returned to the crib and put my head next to Deirdre's.

I was still there when Dad came in and stood by me. I didn't look up. I felt his tears on the back of my hand. And I remembered that he loved children.

15

Deirdre did not die for another two days. It was as if she was waiting for Mum to arrive so that we could all be together. And we were. Deirdre did not open her eyes, but she knew we were there.

And then it was over. The funeral and the tea and sandwiches at the one-and-a-half-story house in West-bury, with the Lavender Lady suffering too much on our behalf and Miss Jessop talking about the garden to Betty; Alan putting his arm around me and saying why didn't I bring Nadine down for Whitsun week and he'd cancel some appointments and teach us how to water-ski; Mum watching me, beautiful in a knitted suit, begging me silently to say yes. And me saying yes. And thanks. And not wriggling away from the strong osteopath's arm.

A week went by. I had a filthy cold and so did Betty. We sat by the fire and watched television. Les McGregor did a one-man show. We laughed a lot at that, and Betty said he was her favorite comedian. Mrs. Pollard looked after the twins and got the meals. "This is heaven," Betty sighed. She meant it.

Mum came to see me. I knew what it must have cost her to come to the farm. I don't expect she'd been back since Deirdre went into the hospital and she shredded away with guilt and terror. She looked beautiful in a linen dress, her blue-tinted glasses taking up most of her face.

"Is it going to be all right, Cass?" She was still frightened. Frightened of me.

I nodded. "Yes. I think so." I screwed up my face to hold back the damned tears. "Mum . . . I'm sorry."

She grabbed at me. She held me tightly. "Darling, you mustn't say that—you mustn't think it. That's how I was. It's only by accepting things as they are that you can *survive*!" She wasn't frightened of me, she was frightened for me.

I said in a voice muffled by her shoulder, "I didn't mean I was sorry about Deirdre. You know I'm not. I'd do it all again. I had to be with her . . . it was right." I drew a deep breath and peeled off another layer of secrets; pretty soon I'd be raw. "I mean I'm sorry about before. Being jealous of you and Alan. Was that why you kept Mark away from me?"

I could feel her surprise, her shock. She put me gently back in my chair, then sat on the edge of hers. "Did I do that? Yes . . . yes, I suppose I did. I wanted Mark . . . for myself."

I could see that hurt her. Maybe she was as raw as I was.

I said, "I wanted Dad for myself. It doesn't work, does it?"

She didn't answer, but after a moment, when I thought she was going to cry, she smiled and put out her hand. I put mine into it.

I said, "Mum, tell me about it. Please. Dad's no good at talking. Even now he can't talk about it. He works like a maniac, plays with the kids, looks after Betty and me as if we're invalids . . . but he can't talk."

Mum sighed. "No. He never could. When Deirdre was born he said, 'It's happened and it's over and we forget it and go on.' And I couldn't forget it. It was with me every minute, even when I was asleep. Guilt and horror and love and loneliness. And they all added up to fear. I was frightened all the time, Cass. Frightened to go outside the door, to stay in the house, to speak to people. . . . The doctor sent me into Bristol. To the psychiatric hospital. You know all that."

I ached with pity. I knew how it had been. Sometimes, this past week, sitting with Betty and being pampered, I had wondered if the madness was still waiting for me. Like Mum said: guilt and horror and love. But not loneliness. Not anymore.

Mum sighed and tried to smile again. "Afterward, when I was better . . . when I told everyone I was better . . . you were so settled with Dad. He's a natural father, is Jack. In a way that is why he had to repudiate Deirdre's very existence. Just as a bird will discard the weakling chick, so Jack . . . I want you to understand why Dad lied to you about Deirdre. It was because he *thought* of her as being dead. His concern was for you, Cass. The living. Both his daughters lived in you, and he gave his time and energy to both of them when he looked after you. Can you understand that?"

"Yes." I remembered Gideon's words. "Yes, I do understand." And I knew suddenly why the madness was not waiting for me after all. Love, guilt and horror. And the strongest of these is love.

Mum's smile became a little more positive. She squeezed my hand. "I didn't come back home, Cass. You know that too. There was Alan. I wouldn't marry him because I was convinced I brought only misery to those I loved. Dad made me see that I was simply dodging life—it was all self-pity. He said, 'Go ahead and marry Alan Forrest. You're not suited to be a farmer's wife. That's all there is to it.' Can't you just hear Dad saying that? 'Not suited' . . . as if it were some job I was resigning from."

I could hear him say that. I *had* heard him say that.

Mum said, "Well, I took his advice and married Alan. But he also advised me to stop seeing Deirdre. And I didn't do that."

I whispered, "I'm glad."

"So am I. Though, believe me, Cass, it didn't get any easier. But . . . she was so like you. She was easy to love."

"Oh, Mum." The tears were there again. For both of us.

We made tea and drank it and listened to the twins laughing somewhere with Betty. I told Mum that Betty loved flowers and helping Dad, and she said, "Yes. Yes, Cass, she is very suited to . . ." She had been going to say "to being a farmer's wife" and suddenly she didn't. She said instead, "She is very suited to being Dad's wife." And I nodded. I accepted at last that they were "suited"—that they were what Mrs. Pollard called "a pigeon pair."

When our tea was finished, Mum said, "Nobody thought Deirdre would live as long as she did, Cass. That was another thing. We didn't think you should know about her because there was so little time."

I thought of her lying there in that crib, twisted, bent, no arms. It was so unfair.

"Why? Why did it happen?" I asked. "And why did she die?"

Mum felt as I did; I could see the pain on her face. It was like a wound; it would heal, but there would always be a scar and occasionally it would nag and ache.

She said in a low voice, "I don't know the answer, Cass. It's called Down's syndrome. When it's severe— as in Deirdre's case—it usually means a short life span. But Deirdre . . . on her good days she could go out. In a chair, of course. She—she loved going out." Mum swallowed convulsively. Had she wheeled Deirdre around a hypermarket, I wondered?

Mum's voice trembled slightly. "Her chest cavity simply wasn't big enough. Only the top half of her lungs worked, anyway. When she went to Worrall Hall, they said two months. Maybe three. Alan decided on a holiday—he thought I would need my—my strength later. If he'd realized . . . Cass, he is a kind, good man. He loved Deirdre. He wants to love you. Believe me. Please."

I was choked again. I believed her. I was very thankful I'd said yes to the water-skiing.

I got up and made more tea. I told her a bit about Gideon and a lot about Nadine and everything about the Lavender Lady. She said that Mrs. Rossen-Phillips visited Deirdre's hospital regularly and what a blessing it had been when her final transfer had been to Worrall Hall, so close to Mrs. R.-P.'s home. "I couldn't have gone off to Ibiza otherwise," Mum said. "But Deirdre loved that woman. And her housekeeper, Miss Jessop."

I said hoarsely, "They loved her too. So did that Sister in the hospital." I cleared my throat and spoke very clearly. "So did I."

We drank the tea. I noticed that Mum's glasses were

askew and her lipstick was smudged. She was still beautiful.

When it was time for her to go, she said, "I'm glad it happened the way it did. We were wrong to keep Deirdre a secret." She smiled a lovely upside-down smile. "Mark sends his love. He says don't forget the pact."

I said, "Tell him I've still got my half."

When our colds were almost better, Dad came into the sitting room in his muddy boots and told us what he thought about layabouts who sat drinking tea and watching television all day.

He said, "I want you to get in touch with that Jones chap, Cass. And Nadine too, if she can stop giggling for two minutes. Tell them to get themselves up here on weekends and after college. I can't expect Betty to give me a hand this summer, and it will take three of you to replace her."

Betty flushed and tucked her chin into her neck. I said mildly, "Okay, Dad. It will give me a reason for phoning them, I suppose."

"Do you all good to get out on the land and work some of your nonsense out of you," Dad grumbled. "I know you're not keen on farm work, Cass, but you've got a feeling for our Mendip. Get out with Mendip, girl. She can do more for you than anything. Just you remember that."

Every year a band of ragged pilgrims comes to Glastonbury Tor and talks about the rhythms of the earth. I think that was the sort of thing Dad had in mind. Nadine would like it.

She did. I rang her that night, and when I told her what Dad had said, she started sniffling over the wires.

"What's the matter with you?" I said, surprised.

"Just that your Dad . . . I was thinking of him all those years ago. Looking after you. Working. Getting close to the land. He's a lovely man, Cass."

"Yes." I thought about it. "Yes, he is. Thanks, Naddie."

She gulped and then said hardily, "Call me Naddie just once more and I kill you."

"How?"

"Give you my ingrown toenails."

We couldn't stop. Laughing, I mean. Dad moaned about what the phone bill would be for giggling. Betty said, "But they're *girls*, Jack. Girls are *supposed* to giggle!"

The Lavender Lady wanted to talk. She wanted so much to take me under her wing and help me and look after me and encourage me to visit hospitals for the mentally handicapped with her. But Miss Jessop knew better. She let Betty show her the garden, and then she came in and put a firm hand on Mrs. Rossen-Phillips's shoulder.

"Plenty of work here, Rowena," she said sternly. "I think Catherine is going to be very busy indeed.

Perhaps she and her young man could find time to come to tea after the hay is in?"

So it was fixed. Perhaps one day I will go to those hospitals with the Lavender Lady. Not yet.

Finally Gideon. Nadine phoned him for me to ask him about helping on the farm. I expected him to call me then, but he didn't. Instead, the next evening after college, he turned up at the back door in his decent jeans, with his helmet under one arm and his eyes very direct.

Dad said, "It's all right. No words necessary. Take her for a walk up the coombe."

I bundled him off before he could start calling Dad "sir." We climbed up to my special rock and looked at all that land around us, and he asked me if I was all right.

I said, "When I was small, I played a game sometimes. I pretended I was a bird and I could fly all over this land. Wells. Glastonbury. The lakes. I'd swoop over the Levels and down to Weston. I'd follow the Severn as far as the Bridge. I never went any farther. That was my territory. It would be dangerous to go into foreign lands."

Gideon said uncertainly, "Are you trying to tell me something, Cass? Did we do wrong to find out about Deirdre?"

"No. I think I'm trying to say I couldn't have done it on my own. You . . . kept me up. Flying."

"I don't want gratitude from you, Cass."

"What do you want?"

He didn't answer, and at last I turned from that map view and looked at him. He was frowning, but when he met my eyes he—completely unexpectedly— *laughed!*

"Oh, Cass. Words again. You've got me trapped, haven't you? I could have answered that question very easily at Easter. Now . . . I don't know what I want. Christ, I still want you. Like hell. But not the way it was before. And anyway, if you belonged to me, that would tie you down in some way. I don't want to see you tied down, Cass. I want to see you flying again. Belonging to all of this." He swept the air with a grandiose arm.

I looked at the view again so that he couldn't see my smug grin.

"What you're trying to say," I remarked flatly, "is that you don't want to help get the hay in next month."

He started to splutter protests, then stopped, then laughed again.

"I'm beginning to know you, Cass. And . . . you know me."

I let him see my grin. We laughed together. "You're good at the grand gesture," I told him. I sobered. "Good for me that you are."

We looked again at our special land mass. He said, "What do *you* want, Cass?"

"A quiet life. Seriously. I don't want any more hassle. I want to finish college and get a job. I want to be with Mark and the twins. I want to share Betty's new baby—she'll let me now. I want to love Mum and Dad. Get to know Alan. Be crazy with Nadine." I paused. "I'd like to see a lot of you, Gideon. If that's all right."

"That's all right."

I felt in my pocket and drew out the contents and laid them on the flat rock in front of us. A shoelace. Two fluffy ears from a toy rabbit. He didn't know about the shoelace, but he knew about the rabbit. He took one of the ears very slowly and diffidently, as if waiting for a protest from me. When he got none, he put it in his pocket.

"Tell you one thing I *don't* want, Gideon." I hung on to the other ear. "I don't want Deirdre to be a secret. Not ever again."

His smile was beautiful. Gentle and beautiful. "How could she be when you're alive, Cass?"

It was a difficult concept, and he'd put it so simply. The idea of living for someone else could be a responsibility . . . a morbid responsibility. But I knew, looking at Gideon, that I felt freer, more complete, than I had ever felt before.

We walked back down the coombe side by side. I was conscious of every bit of my body and I was grateful for it. And very proud that I looked like my sister.

Oh my dove, that art in the clefts of the rock, in the secret places of the stairs, let me see thy countenance, let me hear thy voice; for sweet is thy voice, and thy countenance is comely.
—The Song of Solomon

About the Author

SUSAN SALLIS was born in England and taught school for several years after graduating from the College of Education in Bristol. She has written for a variety of magazines and has had several books published, including A TIME FOR EVERYTHING, AN OPEN MIND, and ONLY LOVE.

She and her husband live in Avon, England. They have three children.